Frozen Fate

Marcie Harris

Contents

Chapter 1

I 've been accepted.

I stared at the piece of paper in my hand and re-read the same sentence over and over again trying to let this odd piece of information sink in. How was I accepted to this university? I never applied for it, I've never even heard of this place.

I shuffled through the papers and saw the crest of the university on the top of the acceptance paper – Abled University. I furrowed my eyebrows at the name, kind of name is that for a university? I ran through all the names I could remember of the universities I wanted go to be accepted to and Abled University was not one of them.

I jumped off the kitchen stool I'd been sitting on and walked towards the lounge. Sitting on the sofa was Troy with Serena lying down with her legs flung across his lap. Troy and Serena were my parents' best friends and raised me up as their own daughter after my parents were killed in a car crash while I was a baby.

"Hey guys, can I ask you a question?" I asked them. They turned their heads at the sound of my voice and switched the television off to give me their full attention. This was something I loved about them. They weren't even blood related to me and yet they loved me and treated me as though they were my own mom and dad. They were amazing god parents.

"What's up Shrimp?" Troy asked.

"Come on, really? I've had my growth spurt already, no need to call me Shrimp anymore!" I complained but rolled my eyes anyway and continued waving the papers in front of their faces, "Well, I received this acceptance letter but I never-"

"OH MY GOD! You're finally going! You're finally going to Abled University!" Serena screamed effectively cutting me off and grabbed the acceptance papers jumping around like a lunatic. Her high pitched squeals were ignored as Troy stood up.

"Congratulations!" he said while giving me a fatherly hug.

"Err, thanks?" I said making it sound more like a question. "But how did I get accepted if I never even applied for it? I've never even heard of the place! Did you guys have something to do with this?"

They both obviously knew the place so I was curious how I was secretly accepted. Serena had calmed down by now and wrapped me in a tight hug before sitting down in Troy's lap. I smiled. Serena was youngish for a guardian but was even younger at heart, sometimes making me feel like the more mature one sometimes.

"No sweety, we didn't have anything to do with it... but your parents did" she answered my question with unshed tears brimming in her eyes. I froze... my parents?

"My parents? How... how is that possible?" I stammered.

"Maybe you should sit down sweety" Serena suggested. Her childish attitude was gone and she was completely serious as she looked me in the eye ready to answer all my unanswered questions. I sat down and leaned in close. "You remember the talk I had with you about your water abilities?" I nodded.

Ever since before I could remember I'd always loved the water; anything to do with water from swimming in the ocean to washing dishes. Whenever I was surrounded by water I couldn't help but feel completely serene and at peace. If I was upset or stressed it would soothe me almost like a comforting embrace between a mother and her child.

At the age of 16 I realised I was able to move water, to manipulate the moisture in the air and was even able to freeze just by the simplest movements. I completely freaked out and ran to Serena thinking I was going completely nuts but she calmed me down and explained what I was – I was 'Water-abled'. She then continued to explain to me that she and even my mother were Water-abled and that there were many others in the world who were. As well as people who had different abilities.

My mind came back to reality and wondered what my water abilities had to do with anything so I let her continue. "Well, Abled University is the university your parents and I went to when we were younger. It's the university for the Abled – people with extra-ordinary abilities." Serena explained. "You didn't have to apply for the university because it was always planned that you were to go attend Abled University."

I didn't say anything. I just sat on the sofa letting all this new information sink in: I was going to go to the university my parents went to. Maybe I could find out more about them? I felt my heart beat faster in excitement at being able to learn more about this side of my parents. I'd always been curious about them and would always ask Troy and Serena to tell me stories about them. They would tell me anything about them yet they always managed to avoid answering any questions about my parents' abilities.

"Well then I'm definitely going" I smiled, "I wouldn't ever pass the opportunity to make my parents proud, even if they're not here."

The weeks passed quickly and before I knew it I was all packed and ready to leave home and move into Abled University. I was lucky enough that the university was only a few hours drive away so I would still be able to visit Troy and Serena from time to time.

"I can't believe you're leaving! You're growing up so quickly! Oh my little Valerie!" Serena was crying and hugging my head as she started recounting the days when she first saw me as a baby. I shot a panicked look at Troy with an expression that screamed 'GET HER OFF ME!!! SHE'S A BLOODY NUTCASE!!!'

I was still trying to pry Serena's fingers from my face as she began sobbing about my first day of school and Troy just stood by laughing at us and taking photos on his camera.

"Serena! For heaven's sake, she'll be back when she's on holidays, let the poor girl go!" he laughed and blew a raspberry on the side of her neck. She squealed, successfully letting me go, and hit Troy on the shoulder.

"Oh my God! I can breathe!" I cried dramatically sucking in air.

"You guys are bullies" Serena pouted with a ghost of a smile playing on her lips.

I smiled and gave her a hug. I'd miss Troy, of course, but Serena and I were closer and she was really more of a sister than a mother-figure. She'd been my best friend for years and now I was moving away to a place where I knew no one, starting completely fresh. My nerves were buzzing through me and yet at the same time excitement course through my veins.

"I'll come back on my holidays, I promise!" I gave both of them a kiss on the cheek and hopped into my red convertible. Serena and Troy had bought it for me for my eighteenth birthday which would be in a few days and since I was spending it away from home they surprised me earlier. It wasn't brand new. It was a car that I would say had 'character'.

"Love you guys! Keep Serena in check Troy, I'm handing over the responsibility to you!" I laughed as Serena pouted again. Troy waved at me with a smile and cuddled Serena from behind linking his fingers together and resting his head on her shoulder.

I started the engine and drove onto the road. I glanced into the side mirror and felt my heart clench at seeing my godparents grow smaller and smaller the farther I drove.

When they finally were too far to see, I sucked in a big breath and exhaled finally realising that I was on my own.

"Wow…"

That was all I could say when I drove up to the university. It was a huge! The old building reminded me of the school in X-Men where all the 'gifted' people went. I snorted, well that was just ironic, I thought. It stood tall and was built of grey bricks that had crumbled slightly over the years and had vines creeping up between the cracks. It looked as though it was from another era altogether.

I parked my car and grabbed my purse before I walked inside to find my dorm so I knew where I was going before I started to unload. The whole campus was buzzing with students moving in and I was surprised at how normal they all looked. I didn't know what I expected exactly. It's not like I thought people would be throwing balls of water or fire and shifting the ground but I guess the normality of everything surprised me.

I breathed in the fresh air as I walked to the administration. The chatter and laughter of the students around me made me feel more and more excited. The lady at the administration sorted through a list of dorms and stuck a small piece of paper in my hand and a set of keys. I quickly glanced at the white sheet of paper and found out my room was number 427.

My eyebrows quirked at the number scribbled down. How many rooms were there in this place exactly? I walked back to my car to grab some of my luggage. I had packed my whole life into several boxes and bags so I knew I would be making more than one trip to empty out my car.

I made my way to the elevators and pressed the fourth floor, I was struggling to carry my purse and three other bags slung over my shoulders as well as a huge box I could barely see over and I quickly realised my mistake of grabbing too much luggage. The elevator dinged and I walked out turning the corner only to bump against a wall.

I bounced back and the weight of my bags and the box were too much to balance and I ended up falling to the ground dropping everything on top of me with a muffled 'oomph'.

"Hey! Watch where you're going!" I hear a deep voice growl. I looked up and saw that the wall I bounced was, in fact, a gorgeous guy. He was easily the most handsome guy I'd come across, with his raven black hair and olive skin. What entranced me though were his golden eyes, almost like melted gold, with flecks of onyx in them. Even from sitting on the ground I could tell he was well over six foot and the aura that surrounded him screamed 'mysterious'.

The only thing that ruined him was his attitude. I stood up brushing off non-existent dust from my legs and denim shorts before staring him straight in the eye.

"No, I think you should watch where you're going. I was walking with a stack of bags and a box nearly half the size of me! As if you didn't see me!" I growled back. I mean, he may be God's gift to women but I hated being spoken down to as if he was king of the university.

However, by the time I finished talking he was already walking away and I was stuck gazing at the muscles rippling under his white t-shirt. "Hey, are you ok?" I hear another male voice ask.

I turned around and saw another handsome guy with sandy blonde hair and brown eyes looking at me with concern. Unlike the mysterious jerk, I immediately felt at ease around this guy.

"Yeah, I'm all good" I replied nonchalantly.

"Good" he smiled, "I saw you and Derrek bump into each other and him walk off."

I rolled my eyes, great I didn't think anyone saw that...

"Mmm... yeah." I said. There really wasn't much else to say to that.

"Need some help?" he asked, but didn't wait for a reply from me before bending down to lift all my bags and the box while handing me my purse. "What room are you in?"

"Uhh, room 427" He nodded and continued walking down the corridor I was walking down. Well at least I was going the right way. "My name's Valerie, but you can call Val" I said turning to offer him a grateful smile.

"Oh sorry, I always forget to introduce myself to new people. It's nice to meet you Val, the name's Max" he grinned. I laughed and we continued walking while dodging the other students who crowded the hallway. It was much easier for me squeeze through the crowds of moving students now that Max was bulldozing his way through them using my luggage to pry the crowd apart.

"So Max, you said earlier that I bumped into Derrek. How do you know him?" I asked curiously.

"Well he and I were on the same football team in high school and now we're room-mates, speaking of which... this is my room so if you ever need anything, I'm your guy" Max told me nodding his head at room 420.

"Cool, thanks." There was even less of a chance I'd go to his room now that I knew this Derrek character was sharing a room with him. Prick.

"Here we are, room 427. Got your key Val?" Max asked.

I took the key from my pocket and unlocked the door opening it wide enough for Max to walk through. I followed after him and my eyes widened at the dorm. It was much more than I expected, it was huge. It was all open planned and had a little lounge area with a couch, coffee table and TV, as well as a kitchen area that was separated by a counter. On the other side of the lounge there was a balcony and to my left was a closed door which I assumed was the bedroom.

What stood out from everything, however, were the many plants that inhabited the room. My eyes grazed over the different coloured flowers that seemed to grow almost everywhere and little green house plants that sat upon tables or shelves. There were also vines that crept up the frames of the doors that instantly softened the modern look of the room to a softer , more natural one. I stifled a laugh when I saw there was, what looked like, a real tree growing in the corner of the room.

The tree's thick trunk wedged its way up the corner and once it reached the ceiling the branches spread out dangling its beautiful green leaves from the ceiling. "Uh... please tell me your room is like this as well..." I asked Max just staring the tree.

"Um, nope sorry. Your room sure has... character?" he answered scratching his head in confusion.

Just then the bedroom door opened and a short girl appeared with a huge smile painted on her face.

"Hi! You must be Valerie, I'm Helena your new roommate" she greeted me in her warm voice before wrapping me in a hug. "Oh is this your boyfriend?" she asked looking at Max whose cheeks flushed red.

"Oh no, no, no we just met in the corridor. He's helping me with my things." I explained.

"Oh okay, well I'm all finished unpacking so if you have more things I can help you out too" she volunteered.

"Sure thanks!"

I immediately loved Helena. She seemed to have this personality that just sucked you in and automatically made you believe you'd been friends since before time began. She was very short and petite with long wavy brown hair with sun kissed blonde streaks. Her skin had a Mediterranean skin tone and had kind brown eyes.

As Max and Helena helped me bring all my boxes up from my car I asked Helena why our room was like a forest when the other rooms clearly weren't.

"Oh don't you just love it? I'm Earth-abled so I can influence the earth and all plant life." She explained. Well, that totally explained everything! "What are you?" she asked cocking her head to the side with a smile.

"I'm Water –abled, so looks like we'll get along just peachy" I grinned back at her. Her smile grew and agreed with me.

"Hey you're Water-abled? So am I!" Max cried happily. I hi-fived him and we continued unpacking my belongings.

I'm loving it here already!

Chapter 2

Max and I sat side by side on the sofa, completely exhausted from unpacking everything I owned and were watching Helena dance around the floor as she worked her earth abilities on the plants. It was amazing to watch as the vines slithered around the banisters and the flowers bloomed just that little bit more to brighten up the atmosphere.

The sun shone through the balcony door and a light breeze rustled the leaves of the plants. The apartment continuously had a beautiful floral scent that lingered in my nose and I was finding it very calming.

"Aw you need a little more sunlight" Helena cooed to a potted plant before she placed it on the balcony, "Ooh and you look a little thirsty" she murmured to another potted flower.

I smiled and waved my fingers, feeling the water molecules gather between my fingertips, then as I saw the little ball of water appear I pushed my hand towards the flower and the ball of water travelled over the top of it. I spread my fingers apart and the ball sprinkled down like a mini liquid cloud raining over the beautiful petals.

"Ooh! That was amazing Val!" Helena clapped. "I'm so happy you're my room-mate! "

I grinned at her enthusiasm and Max applauded me. "You seem like you have a lot of control over your abilities Val" Max pointed out. I shrugged my shoulders and smiled, I wasn't used to having people compliment me on my abilities when it was something I kept quiet before coming to Abled University.

"So Val, how old are you?" Helena asked sitting down, finally finished with her plants.

"I'm eighteen on Saturday, how about you guys?"

"What! It's your birthday on Saturday?! We have to have a party! It'll be like a 'happy birthday/get to know everyone party'"

I actually hadn't even thought about it but it sounded like an awesome idea so Max and I quickly agreed and I started deciding on getting food and drinks while Max and Helena would spread the word. I was excited about everything and it seemed like Helena's enthusiasm was extremely contagious.

"Let's go Max, we only have two days to let everyone know about this party!" Helena urged while practically jumping from one foot to the other in the door way. He laughed and rolled his eyes.

"Ok, ok I'm going. I'll catch you later Val" he said giving a quick wave of his fingers before Helena pulled him out into the corridor screaming 'PARTY AT ROOM 427 ON SATURDAY!'

I chuckled to myself before I gathered my keys and purse, checking inside if I had my wallet, then locked up before heading to the bottle shop and the groceries for the snacks.

"Val what do you think of this one?" Helena asked me as she twirled around showing off her loose flowing halter top constructed from several layers of shimmery chiffon. It had different hues of green and gave of a hippie kind of look. She wore denim shorts underneath and finished her look with strappy green wedges.

"It's absolutely perfect Helena" I gushed. Her hair was tumbling down her back in beautiful curls and her make up was done to perfection.

She blushed then froze. "Val! Why the heck aren't you ready yet?"

"Because you said, and I quote, 'Val, drop everything you are doing right now and help me please!'" I laughed as I did a bad imitation of Helena's voice.

She scrunched her nose and giggled, "Oh... woopsies!"

I laughed then moved over to my wardrobe flinging a sapphire blue dress onto my bed. I could hear Helena cooing over my dress and I chuckled, she was too cute sometimes. I showered then slipped on the dress noticing it fit a little snugger than I remember. I guess I really should back off the boredom eating.

"Done, done and done" I announced spinning around for Helena to see.

"How the hell can you look like that in just twenty minutes? I'm so jealous!" Helena gushed.

We hurried out of our room to make sure we enough of everything and that the music was pumping already. Helena and Max told everyone that the party started at nine and it was getting close to it already.

A knock came from the door and Max burst through looking mighty fine and with his arms full with extra drinks. "Can I drop these here?" he asked with a strained voice but dropped them on the counter anyway. I always wondered why he bothered asking when he knew it was fine and did it anyway. I laughed and shook my head.

"Wow Val, you look... wow, so beautiful" he said as he stared at me. I winked and looked him up and down. He wore slightly loose fitted jeans with a sky blue button down long sleeve shirt with the sleeves rolled up to his elbows and white sneakers, the look suited him well.

"You don't look half bad hot shot" I replied.

The sound of someone clearing their throat interrupted us and we saw Helena playfully crossing her arms.

"Guys! Don't leave me out now!" she pouted making us laugh.

"Helena, you look absolutely outstanding, no stunning, no breath taking!" Max cried playfully placing his hand over his heart.

His outburst made us burst into laughter but that too was interrupted by the knocking coming from the door. I could hear the muffled sound of voices from the other side and a my lips curved into a large grin. "Looks like the party has arrived"

The party was booming and so many people turned up we eventually had to leave the door open letting the party spread out to the corridor. I was getting greeted and congratulated on throwing such a great party and even had a few guys ask me to dance with them. The usually big apartment felt cramped with the amount of people squashing together and the floral scent had been replaced by the scent of sweat and alcohol.

"Hey Val! Can we go somewhere quieter!" Max shouted into my ear. The music and people were so loud it came out as though he was just talking to me. I nodded, not bothering to try to shout back, and took his outstretched hand. We trudged through the crowd of partiers and finally he was able to pulled me outside the apartment and walked down towards his room.

"Crazy party eh?" he huffed.

"You're telling me! I can barely hear myself think anymore!" I replied, "Where are we going by the way?"

"My room, I have something to give you." He tugged me again and pushed open his door. We walked into his apartment, which would have looked exactly the same for mine minus the forest of plants, then into his and Derrek's room. It had that distinct 'boy smell' and was actually cleaner than I thought it would be. Kudos to them.

"Here" he called to me. I turned and saw him holding out a little delicate box with a blue ribbon carefully wrapped around.

"Aw Max, you seriously didn't need to!" I tried to say but he waved me off instead telling me to open it.

I slid the ribbon off and opened the velvet box. Inside was a necklace with a sapphire pendant in the shape of a tear drop, there was a fine wire of silver wrapping around it in an elaborate fashion and it was absolutely beautiful. I'd never seen anything like it before.

"Max... it's beautiful! Can you put it on for me?" I held it out to him and turned around. He fiddled with the lock and secured it around my neck brushing his smooth fingers down the top of my spine.

"I saw it and thought it suited you perfectly" he told me. He was looking straight into my eyes and leaning forward. I could tell he was going to kiss me but I leaned back sending him a nervous smile.

"Sorry... I shouldn't have-" he started to say.

"No, no it's ok Max. It's just... I only just met you, you know?" I cleared my throat, "So uh... where's your room –mate?"I asked sneering on 'room-mate' a little.

His chuckle broke the awkward atmosphere and he rubbed his hands over his hair. "He's at your party Val, didn't you see him?"

I furrowed my eyebrows. How did I not see Derrek? Obviously there were plenty of people there but still... I should have at least glanced at him once. Oh well, I thought, it wasn't as though he was important.

"Nope" I shrugged, "But speaking of which, we should probably head back there."

He nodded and slipped his arm around my shoulders leading me back to the raging party. I almost forgot what it was like to have my brain bounce around my skull from the bass but alas, I now remembered.

I joined in a few drinking games, drank some shots, danced with Helena and Max then drank more shots. I was buzzing and pretty sure I couldn't feel my toes anymore. I was laughing hysterically at something Max said, but couldn't for the life of me remember what it was, when I was offered another shot.

Before I could throw back the liquid Max stopped me.

"Wait Val, just wait!" he screamed with a grin.

He ran to the ipod and paused the music resulting in a chorus of boos and 'what the hell's?!'

"Ev-everyone grab a shot!" he yelled slurring horribly, everyone grabbed one and waited to see what he was going to say next, "I just wanna say HAPPY BURFDAY to the burfday girrrl! And on the count of... on the count of threeeee we all say happy burfday then take the shot!"

I was laughing at the drunken mess he was and had to hold on to Helena when he started belting out 'Happy Birthday' way, way off pitch. He was swaying around and if I wasn't drunk I would have run up to ensure he didn't fall face first on the ground. When he finished singing, he started to shout -

"ONE! TWO! TWO AND A HALF! TWO AND THREE FIFTHS! TWO AND ANOTHER BIT!"

Someone yelled for him to get on with it.

"Ok fine.... party pooperrrrr. THREEEEEEEEE!!!!" He yelled. He skulled his shot a little too eagerly and fell over backwards completely passed out. Everyone downed their shots at same time, only for some to spit it out when he fell over to burst out in hysterics, and thankfully someone pressed play on the ipod.

I was practically on the floor with Helena crying with tears of laughter at Max's display and figured he'd be out for the rest of the night, and probably all tomorrow. People had left a circle around his unconscious body as they continued to dance and mingle so it would be easy enough to reach him.

"Helena! H-Helena! Help me get Max onto my bed!" I screamed.

"Oooh-kayyy!" she sang back and we pushed our way through the grinding bodies to Max who was sprawled out on the floor.

Both of us were giggling and dragging Max under the arm pits towards our room, which was blocked by vines from the inside so no one could sneak a little private time in our room. Luckily Max was passed out close to it otherwise we'd probably give up and leave him there. The guy was so huge and heavy it took both of us just to struggle with him.

"Helena unblock the door" I slurred to her.

She released her hold on Max making me slump under his weight as he bumped his head on the floor. Helena was so drunk she was wiggling her hands at the door like the witches in old movies, making me laugh even more.

Apparently the vines moved because she opened the door and we continued to struggle to get him on the bed. He was way too heavy and we ended up leaving him on the floor between our beds, shoving a pillow under his head and throwing a blanket over him.

"Gooooodnight Maxy Waxy" Helena cooed patting him on the head like a baby.

We left the room and blocked it again with vines. I was starting to sober up so I threw back a few more shots and then mixed vodka with mango juice in a cup. Helena was dancing in the middle of the swaying bodies so I pushed my way to her and started dancing with her again.

I felt a warm body dance behind me and big hands grip my hips as I swayed side to side. I caught Helena's eye and silently asked if he was cute. Her facial expression replied 'ouchy mama, that is one hot papacito', so I smiled and leaned back into him sneaking a look over my shoulder.

Hmm... not too bad. He had that surfy guy look going on and I was pretty sure I'd danced with him a few times during the night. The alcohol was hitting me hard again and I emphasized my movements back against him throwing my arm around his neck and leaning my head back onto his shoulder.

"Let's go get some fresh air babe" he shouted into my ear. I nodded lazily and let him tug my hand towards the surprisingly empty balcony.

I slumped onto a plastic sun lounge closing my eyes and felt my arms go floppy. I was pretty close to passing out I'm sure. Suddenly I felt hot wet lips on my neck and sweaty hands on my chest. I jerked awake and tried to push whoever this guy was off of me.

"Go away..." I slurred loudly.

"Come on babe, I know you want it. You've practically been begging for it all night" He laughed darkly. I was getting scared and no matter how hard I tried to push him off, my lack of strength and drunken state was in his favour.

"Help!" I cried when I felt my dress bunch up and his knee push my legs apart. Oh God please don't let this happen! "Please! Someone! Anyone!" I screamed, tearing pouring down my face as I uselessly tried to push him off. His weight was starting to crush me and I was losing my breath.

The music was too loud, no one can hear me. No one's going to help me...

"Shut up! You want this!" Was all I heard before a sharp sting made contact across my cheek. My vision blurred and I noticed a dark silhouette behind this pathetic excuse of a man on top of me.

"Help..." I whispered.

All of a sudden the man's weight was pulled off of me and I heard a distinctive 'oompf'.

I rolled off the blasted sun lounge and peeked over the arm rest to see someone beating the living crap out of the pathetic assaulter. The guy doing the punching let the unconscious body drop and walked over to me.

"You ok?" A deep voice asked me. It was a sexy voice and even through my hazy state I recognised the voice but couldn't place it.

"I'm ok, thank you so much" I whispered.

He bent down and scooped me up placing me back on the stupid sun lounge. I gasped when I saw it was Derrek who was helping me. I guess he wasn't a complete jerk like I thought he was, go figure. He placed a bent finger under my chin and turned it side to side inspecting my face.

I was completely hypnotized by his beautiful molten gold eyes with swirling onyx flecks. He pressed a finger to my left cheek and I winced. Ow, what the hell was that?

"Stay here, I'll grab you some ice" he whispered to me before heading inside. I sat uncomfortably on the sun lounger darting glances all around me, it was just me and an unconscious prick on the ground, not even awkward. I hope it rains... not just a little sprinkle of raindrops but the ground shaking thunderstorms that spits out rain like a bad taste and he gets soaking wet. I should lock him outside because there's no way I'm dragging his assaulting behind inside.

Derrek came back holding a plastic cup with ice inside and gently pressed it to my cheek. I winced at the contact. "Sorry..." he apologised.

"I'll be ok. I'm just tired I guess..."

We both looked inside at the still ongoing party. "Looks like this won't be over for a while" I huffed leaning back into the seat taking the cup from him and holding it to my face. He smirked and chuckled.

"Want me to get them out of there?" He asked.

"And how would you do that, may I ask?"

"I have my ways" He replied with a smirk as he lifted his hand. He clenched them making a claw shape with his palm facing upwards and a small purple flame burst in the centre of his hand. I gasped and pressed myself back into the seat even more.

"Wow!" I gasped staring at the swirling purple flames, "Um, no I think I'll just let them party it out. No need for... fire.

Besides I really don't think my room-mate would appreciate her plants being toasted."

I watched as he played with the fire, throwing it from one hand to the other as though it was a ball. I guess I knew what his abilities were now.

"Why is it purple?" I asked curiously.

He looked at me raking his gaze down my body. It was making me feel uncomfortable so I shifted and pulled my dress down trying to cover more of my thighs. He chuckled and I could feel the vibrations of his laughter run through me.

"The fire changes colour according to my emotions." He stated matter-of-factly.

"Really? What colours are there and what do they mean?"

"Well, there's purple" he started nodding towards the purple flame he was twirling around, "then there's orange, red and blue. They're the ones I know of at least" he shrugged.

When he didn't continue I asked him –

"And what do they mean?" I urged him.

He smirked and closed his hand letting his fingertips touch causing the flame to disappear leaving a ring of smoke floating up into the air.

"That's for me to know..."

"...and me to find out?" I finished for him.

"Maybe" He stood up and eyed me again.

"Well I'm going to dump this guy somewhere and head off." He stated.

I felt a little sad that he was leaving but I really just wanted to strip off this uncomfortable dress, pull on some sweats, a tank top and pass out on my bed for the next two days. Instead I offered him a smile and only noticing now that he looked yummy in low rise jeans, a white t-shirt and a leather jacket over the top.

He grabbed the unconscious guy's leg and began pulling him inside pausing when the guy's head bumped on the slight dip of the entrance.

"Oops." He said sarcastically. I smiled at his antics and noticed the party had died somewhat, leaving only the passed out or swaying drunk people. I leaned against the front door crossing my arms and watched him leave.

"Thank you again Derrek, for everything." I sighed. He smirked again and winked at me before turning around and heading down the corridor dragging the still unconscious body. Just before he was out of sight he turned around and met my gaze.

"Oh... happy birthday, Valerie."

Chapter 3

Oh God... I feel like death warmed over!

I pried my eyes open and squinted as the bright rays of sunlight streamed through the opened curtains. What the hell happened last night? I was sprawled half across my bed and half on the ground with my sheets tangled between my legs as though I had a fight with them in my semi-unconscious state.

The bad thing was that I didn't realise this before I tried to stand and fell completely off the bed, face first.

"Good morning roomie!" Helena sang with a bright smile plastered to her face. I groaned loudly and quickly covered my ears. It felt like I'd been trampled on by a heard of angry bulls and a marching band were practising in my ear drums!

"Helena! For the love of God, and I say this with complete love... Shut up!" I whisper yelled to her as I slowly, very, very slowly picked myself up from the ground and held a hand to my throbbing head.

She ducked her head and giggled cheekily. "Woopsies! I'm sorry, I forgot you drank enough alcohol to dry out a country last night"

Yeah, that would explain the overwhelming hangover from hell...

"So did you if I recall correctly. Why the hell aren't you puking your guts into the toilet bowl?" I wondered loudly. She was just as drunk as I was and yet here she stood, nothing short of a bloody ball of bouncy sunshine.

She shrugged and skipped over to water her flowers by her bed, "I'm Earth-abled so I don't really get hungover. I think it's in the genes of or something" I heaved a sigh wishing I was Earth-abled as well.

"I'm going to take a shower. I must look like a zombie right now" I told her quietly, though what I really wanted to do was bury myself in my bed sheets and sleep until tomorrow or until the sun was no longer trying to kill my eyes.

I walked into the bathroom glancing in the mirror as I passed and screamed when I did a double take, which was possibly the worst thing for me to do while hungover. Apparently, I had enough sense to pour myself into more comfortable clothes last night but neglected to remove my make up resulting in me looking like that psycho zombie clown from Zombieland.

"Val! Are you ok?!" I heard a muffled Helena yell from the other side of the door.

"I'm fine, I just scared myself" I replied as I caught my breath. I don't know how the hell she didn't collapse in a fit of laughter when she saw me. I finished my shower feeling much fresher and a little less like a corpse. I threw on a yellow tank top and white denim short shorts before letting my hair air dry.

"I'm so hungry!" I moaned clutching my protesting stomach. I walked into the kitchen and decided on cooking up a greasy brunch. "Want some food Helena?" I shouted.

"Ooh! Yes please! I can't cook without burning anything so this only makes you an even better roomie!" She gushed. I chuckled at her answer. Helena was nothing short of a ball of positive energy on redbull and possibly drugs as well.

The apartment soon began to smell like eggs, bacon, sausages and pancakes and I placed all the food on the counter. Just as I was about to dig in an odd knocking came from the door. I say 'odd' because it was a mixture of knocking and random scraping noises. I frowned as I continued to listen.

"What the hell?" I mumbled under my breath. I turned to Helena to give her my 'what the hell' look but she was already stuffing her face with pancakes, so I stood up and opened the door.

"Argh!"

I quickly jumped back as a bulky Max came flying through the doorway onto the ground. Max? I stared confused at Max who was scrawled at my feet, I was pretty sure we left him on the floor in our bedroom.

"Uh... hello?" I said confused as to how he was outside trying to get back inside our apartment.

"Morning Val" he murmured before picking himself up and offering me a lopsided grin. "I don't usually do this, but I am literally begging you to let me eat some of your food. I could smell it outside and I'm just about this close to dying from this headache" he continued barely holding his fingers apart.

I laughed and shook my head in amusement. "Go ahead"

Apparently, Max had dragged himself back to his room and slept a few more hours on his bathroom floor clutching the toilet. Well, better his than mine, I thought grimly. The rest of the day was spent with Max and I recovering from our hangovers while constantly pleading Helena to not sing so loudly.

I sighed and slumped back into the sofa as I let my eyes roam out to the balcony. Memories of last night and my close assault flooded my hazy mind and I thought of how Derrek saved me. I couldn't stop thinking about him.

Last night had completely changed my mind about him being a jerk and I couldn't stop replaying how sweet he was to me after knocking out that creep. You couldn't judge a book by its cover and I'm glad to read a little of Derrek.

"Well thanks for taking care of me girls but I guess I should get back to my room" Max sighed wistfully.

I perked up a little at his announcement. Max and Derrek shared the same apartment and I figured I should say 'thank you' to him again since I was sober now.

"I'll walk you Max, I need to stretch my legs" I offered. Max nodded his and gave a one shouldered shrug as he stood and stretched out his lean body before we both headed into the corridor. Most of the students from our floor were at the party last night and I figured that was the reason for the completely empty hallway.

We reached his room and Max opened the door letting me walk through first and I immediately spotted a shirtless Derrek lounging on the sofa watching football on the TV.

Wow.

"Max, where the hell did you go all day?" Derrek asked not even bothering to look up from the TV.

"Went over to Val's room, she fed me all day" he answered with a sly grin. I laughed at his boyish 'thank you for taking care of me all day' face and it was only then that Derrek turned his attention away from the TV and set his golden eyes on me. I smiled at him, but was taken aback when his eyes narrowed and he turned back to watch football again.

I quirked my eyebrow as I stared at him, curious at his new (or maybe old) personality. "I'll be right back Val" Max told me before rushing to his bedroom to, I assume by the way he was walking, go to the bathroom.

I stood in the lounge behind the sofa awkwardly not know-ing what to do. Derrek didn't turn around or say anything. It was as though the nice and considerate guy who saved me last night never existed. I furrowed my eyebrows and walked over to the arm rest of the sofa keeping my eyes on the TV and glancing at him every once in a while.

"What are you still doing here?" Derrek asked gruffly.

"Uh, I wanted to come by to say thank you for last night and I had a good time talking with you..." I replied meekly. His attitude was putting me off and I was trying to phrase everything so it didn't come off as rude or as though I clingy.

He snorted and continued to keep his eyes on the tackling men, "Don't mention it. Ever. Now if you don't mind I'm busy. You can let yourself out"

I glared at his handsome face. What the hell was his problem? Was he on his man-period or something, because his mood swings were giving me whiplash! I angrily rolled my eyes and turned on my heel stomping my way over to the door and angrily slamming it closed with excessive force.

"Are you ready for our first day?" Helena asked me as we started walking towards our first class – History.

"Yeah, definitely. I don't really know anything about the history of well, all of this" I replied waving my hand to the wondering students. Some were even playing around with their abilities and it really was a sight to see.

We walked into the lecture theatre and found a couple of seats in the middle. The lecture theatre soon began to fill up with the rest of the students and I lazily doodled cartoons on my notebook while we all waited for the teacher.

Bang!

The whole class jumped as the door slammed opened as it hit the wall behind and was soon followed by an old man with paper white hair sticking up in all directions as though he rubbed his hair with a balloon. He reminded me of the professor from Back to the Future and his fanatical movements only proved my point more.

"Welcome class!" he greeted us waving his arms around, "My name is Mr Arbit and together we shall take a journey back to the past of... The Abled!"

He spoke with such passion that I was immediately drawn into his lesson. He did, in fact, talk just like the guy from Back to the Future, and maybe that was why I found him so interesting.

"The Abled... all of you... what do they have in common?" he asked the class walking back and forth waving a hand to emphasis his words. We all looked around and when no one raised a hand or shouted an answer he continued.

"They are you." He concluded. I stared at him waiting for him to continue or at least explain more but he simply stood with a slight smile on his pale face and gazed around the room. The entire lecture theatre threw each other confused glances and Mr Arbit chuckled lightly.

"Confused?" he continued, "Let us gather all that we know. Who here are Earth-abled?" A large amount of people stuck their hands in the air and Helena raised her hand happily looking around at the other students who shared her ability.

"And who are Water-abled?" I put my hand in the air along with a smaller amount of people and on the other side of the theatre I could see Max lazily holding his hand in the air as he rested his elbow on the plastic arm rest. "Now put your hand up if you're Fire-abled."

I looked around and an even smaller amount of students raised their hands, including Derrek who was lazily leaning back in his chair with his feet up on the chair in front of him. "And who are Healers here?" Mr Arbit continued to ask.

Maybe ten people timidly raised their hands, most of which were female. "And lucky last, who are Stingers?"

No one. A low hum of whispers filled the room though it didn't feel like the giddy gossip hum but the weird daunting kind of hum. I frowned at the unfamiliar name and was at least comforted at the fact that a lot of other students didn't seem to know it either.

"That's right. Earth, Water, Fire-abled and Healers are called The Abled. Years ago there was another category. They were called Body-abled and they consisted of both Healers and Stingers.

"As most of you know, Healers heal the body as well as ease the mind; they are all positive." Mr Arbit's voice dropped low and everyone was paying attention, "Stingers were the opposite. They caused pain. Horrible pain in both body and mind that caused the person feeling the pain wish they would die instead. Both Stingers and Healers were also telepathic.

"The Abled were, and are still, governed by a group of people called The Control. The Control had begun to believe that Stingers were polluting the abilities of the Abled society and had decided to kill off all Stingers and finally get rid of their 'waste of ability'. This brought on what we call 'The Stinger Eradication'"

I listened to Mr Arbit's recount on our history and I was entranced with how much went on and no one even knew. I wriggled forward taking down notes as he went on but too soon he checked his wrist and stopped.

"Well class it seems as though time has flown. I suggest you read about The Stinger Eradication in your text book and we'll take it from there next class. Thank you!"

All the students groaned at the prospect of homework and stood up to leave class, but I was actually quite excited to learn about this lost Abled.

"Pretty crazy stuff, right?" Helena asks me.

"I'd say" Max replies as he joins us.

It was a short day for us with only history so when Helena and Max asked if I wanted to go to the mall I declined. I wanted to know more about these 'Stingers' as Mr Arbit called them. I lugged out the huge history text book and looked for the right chapter before settling down to read, highlighting what seemed more important.

The Stinger Eradication.

The Control declared war on all Stingers. Stingers, with telepathic abilities as well as the ability to physically and mentally harm any life form, were deemed useless yet dangerous. Abled did not participate in non-Abled wars and therefore in day to day life their ability was simply dangerous for any Abled. The Control called Stingers 'pollution to the Abled society' and therefore had to be dealt with.

Although most Abled usually coupled and married with others that were of the same abilities, there were few who married differently. It was usually rare for anyone to marry another with a different ability but almost unheard of for a Stinger to marry anyone besides another Stinger. It was, however, also common for Abled to marry and procreate with non-Abled humans.

Abled couples with the same abilities were naturally well connected with their own 'category' therefore once they procreate their children's abilities were just as strong. For the rare couple who marry with different abilities, their abilities would normally be in harmony with the other, for example a Water-abled and Earth-abled. However when they procreate their children would inherit only one ability.

As mentioned above, it was unheard of for Stingers to couple with anyone besides their own 'category' and therefore it was easier for The Control to discover and locate their whereabouts. The Control recruited all abilities, excluding Stingers, and formed an army.

The army combed through households, forests, malls and buildings. They expanded out to every country and all over the world annihilating every Stinger they came across, using the Healers' telepathy to pick them out. Marriages, families and relationships were torn apart as the army burned, torched, froze and shattered the Stingers. Many were lost, including other Abled, during The Stinger Eradication.

It was World War 3 that only the Abled knew about.

I stopped reading.

"That's horrible" I whispered. Simply due to the fact that Stingers didn't particularly have a positive ability it didn't mean they were evil. Men, women, fathers, mothers and even children were murdered because of a group of people thought they had a waste of an ability. I looked at the page in front of me filled with political and emotionless words that explained a horrifying era and sighed as I wondered how the Abled society would differ had The Stinger Eradication not pushed through.

Chapter 4

I spent the rest of the afternoon reading bits about the Stinger Eradication. I blinked a couple of times to soothe my tired eyes and looked outside the window. The sun was getting low and the birds were retiring to their nests calling out the last of their songs for the day. I stretched my arms and heard my stiff bones click.

I closed my text book and decided I've been cooped inside for a bit too long; I really should've taken up Helena and Max on their mall offer. I grabbed an apple from the counter and locked up the room to go for a walk around the campus seeing as there were still a lot of it I hadn't visited yet.

I walked down the plain corridor nodding and offering a polite smile to the odd student then scowled at Derrek's door as I passed it. I couldn't help but think that I imagined the whole 'him being nice' situation the other night. He was so gentle, thoughtful... he was caring. I shook my head at those thoughts. I was confused and all this thinking was doing nothing except giving me a bad headache.

I reached the elevators and decided against it, instead choosing to take the stairwell. I ran down the flights of stairs relishing the thudding of my heart and the warmth that spread over my body so that by the time I reached the bottom floor I had a slight sheen of sweat on my forehead. I ran the back of my hand across my forehead and headed outside. As soon as I stepped outside I took a big breath of fresh air and smiled, this is exactly what I needed. Solitary time and fresh air.

I'd been walking through the forest of trees that grew beside the campus for about twenty minutes, just letting my mind rest and taking in the sights of nature. Above, colourful birds hid in the foliage and the shadows that the streaming sun cast. The wind that blew through the forest howled softly as they raced through the trunks almost as though I was being accompanied by an invisible wolf.

Whoosh.

Suddenly I stopped and craned my neck to point my ear in the direction of an odd sound. Nothing. I stayed silent but continued walking then stopped once more.

Whoosh.

There it was again! I quietly stalked towards the odd sound, making sure to avoid stepping on anything that could alert whatever was making that sound. The sound was becoming louder and louder and I swear I could feel the temperature rise the closer I got to the sound.

I hid behind a cluster of ancient trees and jumped when the whooshing sound clashed so close to me. I peered around the trees and my eyes widened. It was Derrek.

A shirtless Derrek, I might add.

I let my eyes roam over his body seeing as I didn't see him properly in his room. He was wearing low riding jeans with a hint of his boxers showers on the top and sneakers. Derrek had his eyes closed and with one hand opened in front of him. I had no idea what he was doing. He stood as still as a statue and breathed calmly as though he was meditating.

Suddenly he opened his eyes and twitched his hand wider letting a ball of orange flames curl around his palm and lick around his fingers. The flickering of the flames made the shadows dance over his face and I managed to glance some writing tattooed across his left ribs, but I was too far away to see it properly.

He pulled his arm holding the flame back and using all his strength he launched it against a scorched tree trunk. The flying ball flew past and as it hit the tree trunk it exploded, letting the flames lick itself up the trunk shortly before it died leaving nothing but black trails behind.

I stepped backwards not wanting to disturb him, and just like in those cliché movies my foot landed on a stick and it snapped under my weight. Immediately Derrek conjured another orange flame ball but his stature was stiff. Not like his relaxed posture a moment before, and his eyes narrowed as they gazed around his trying to penetrate the darkness.

"Who's there?" His deep voice demanded to the shadows.

I froze, unsure what to do. Should I reply? Do I stay quiet? Do I just run and pretend as though I was never there?

"I said who's there?!" He repeated even louder.

I cringed at the echoing of his deep voice but slowly and carefully stepped around the cluster of trees into his line of sight. His golden eyes held my blue ones before his posture finally relaxed and he stood up straight.

"And what do I owe this pleasure of meeting you in the woods?" he asked sarcastically.

I don't reply at first, letting my eye follow the bead of sweat that rolled leisurely down his chest but managed to catch a glimpse of the flames that still turned in his hands. I cleared my throat.

"I was just taking a walk to get some fresh air... then I heard a noise so I followed it" I explained simply. I stopped and thought for a second, why was I explaining myself to Derrek? I didn't owe him anything. Since he was acting as though he hadn't helped out the other night then I wouldn't acknowledge it and pretend as though it didn't happen either.

"Mhmm... whatever." He grunted then turned around to continue throwing balls of fire at the dead trunk.

I felt my eye twitch at his rudeness and took a deep breath in through my nose before exhaling slowly out my mouth. His attitude was really starting to tick me off. Seriously, what was his problem?

"What exactly are you doing?" I asked, trying to make my voice more confident than I felt. He tensed his body before flinging the flames at the trunk then wiped his brow.

"I don't see how that's your business sweetheart"

I growled under my breath, now he was just trying to anger me and push my limits. He lit up another flame but I was already collecting the water molecules in the air so by the time he threw the rolling ball of flames I matched him and projected my ball of water towards it. The water made contact with the flames then, instead of distinguishing it, I flicked my hand horizontally cut the air in front of me and the fire was engulfed in ice and fell to the soft ground with a muted thud.

"Hey!" he cried. "What the hell!"

I smirked and turned on my heel to leave but he apparently he didn't want any of that. As quick as a bullet he conjured his flames and hurled it at the tree right beside me. I yelped in surprise then turned to see his grim face starring daggers at me as his lip curled into a crooked smirk.

"What the hell is your problem Derrek! You could have hit me!" I yelled at him. In honesty I was probably exaggerating because the tree was far from me but it still scared me and I could still feel the quick fluttering of my heart.

"You're my problem! You think you can just come waltzing in here, act like a diva then leave when you feel like it? I don't think so"

I stared at him and quirked my eyebrow. He sounded like a five year throwing a temper tantrum.

"You don't own the forest. I have every right to be here as you do!" His overreaction seemed to have hit a nerve because before I know it I was twirling both my arms in a circle above my head like a two handed lasso and, with both hands again, slice downwards like an axe.

A shout reverberated from Derrek as a bucket sized gush of water landed on his head and splashed down his entire body, soaking every bit of him. A laugh gurgled up my throat as I took in his surprised expression but then something, literally, hot happened.

It looked so comical as Derrek's face contorted with rage as his shoulders hunched over in anger and his body was literally steaming. Steam was coming off Derrek in waves like a drop of water on a red hot rock and in a minute or two he was as dry as he was before all of this. I just stared dumbfounded at what happened.

"You'll pay for that" he growled slowly. His eyes seemed to burn a brighter gold as he threw a swirling red flame aimed at my chest.

Focusing all my concentration on the damp air around me I swiped my hand in an arc across my body creating a layer of water that ate the fire ball thrown at me. Steam rose where the fire hit as the wall of water splashed to the ground and I huffed throwing him a scowl.

"Someone has tricks up her sleeve" Derrek stated, more matter-of-factly than sarcastically. I didn't think he expected me to be able to do much.

In honesty I was pretty surprised at how quickly I was able to react. I'd never done anything of that magnitude before, just collecting water molecules to create balls of water then usually freezing it. I even made ice sculptures a few months ago. I looked back at Derrek and he seemed to have calmed down.

Just a bit.

Not really.

"Better run along, tadpole" he jeered with a shooing gesture before turning back to hurl flames back at the blackened tree. I stood staring at him with an eyebrow raised. Someone had some serious mood swing issues...

Nonetheless, I took his absence of trying to burn me alive and spun on my heel back the way I came. I walked through the many trees, twisted roots and bushed and soon came into view of the campus and found it was already dark so I quickened my pace inside to my room.

"Hey Val! Where'd you go?" Helena asked when I closed the front door of our room.

"Just went for a walk. How was the mall?" I replied, deciding for some reason that I didn't want her to know about my encounter with Derrek.

I plopped down on the sofa next to her munching on a packet of chips while she rattled on about what shops she dragged Max into and what was cute and this and that. I zoned out after the first five shops because honestly 'girl talk' actually wasn't really my thing.

It was a few hours later that I managed to escape her recount of Max in 'way too tight skinny jeans' and fell into bed exhausted. I had too many questions bubbling around my mind and as each popped I struggled to come up with a reasonable answer for any of them.

This was a crazy first day of university.

"Come on Val, move your cute little butt and get down here!" Max yelled down the corridor, much to my embarrass-ment.

It was the weekend and Max decided it was high time for us to visit the beach. It was surrounded by water so of course my answer was 'hell yes!'

"Go grab the food and drinks and I'll meet you by the car!" I screamed back. Honestly, I wasn't one of those girls that spent forever to get ready before going out in public but we had just finished classes and I literally just stepped into my room.

I hear him utter a 'hurry up' before grabbing the food and drinks and shutting the door. I sighed and dug around for my midnight blue bikini before throwing my hair up in a messy bun. I quickly tossed on a pair of shorts and a loose shirt that dangled off one shoulder. Just before I ran out, I grabbed my beach bag packed with the necessities and ran down to meet with Max and Helena.

"Damn, took you long enough" Max cried winking at me.

"I call shot gun!" Helena shrieked and we all hopped into Max's jeep to head to the beach.

It was completely refreshing to be around a large amount of water again. Ultimately, I preferred fresh water to salt, but water was water and I raced Max to the ocean. Helena was left to drag everything to our pile of clothes and instead of joining us in the water she decided to lay back and soak up some vitamin D.

While Helena worked on her already glorious tan Max and I were busying ourselves swimming. The beach wasn't too busy and the few people who inhabited the beach were either sun baking or old couples who were slowly making their way across the shallow.

"So how are you liking uni so far?" Max asked me as we lazed about under the shade of the umbrella, Helena having nodded off a little while ago. I wriggled my toes in the warm grains of sand that seemed to be different hues of yellow, white and pink and smiled.

"I like it, it's different but it's been so great. Plus I got to meet you" I softly nudged his shoulder with mine.

"Yeah, I know what you mean" Max replied. We sat in silence just letting ourselves bask in the warmth and feeling the moisture all around us tinted with a hint of salt. "So Val, when did you realise you were Water-abled?"

I dug my fingers into the tiny sand particles playing with the grains letting them fall through my fingers as I remembered the day I found out I could manipulate water before licking my lips and recounting it for him.

I was sixteen and just had a particularly stressful day at school and all I wanted to do was relax at home. Take a bubble bath, maybe read a book and go to sleep early. I was lounging in the tub surrounded by cushioning bubbles with my earphones in listening to music. I had my head tilted back and eyes shut as I let the soothing oils in the water calm my body when I randomly started flicking at the water with my fingers.

The water had cooled way past lukewarm temperature already so when I opened my eyes to step out of the tub my eyes widened in surprise. I gasped at the unnatural sight before me. Droplets of water were floating in the air, just gliding slowly around or hovering in the same spot, as though it were floating in space.

At first I was too shocked to move. I just gaped at the image before me before snapping out of the trance I was in. I shook my head and began screaming, what else could I do? At the sound of my screaming the water droplets fell to the ground, pitter-pattering on the tiles like my own personal rain. I grabbed a towel and wrapped it around me before screaming "Serena!" and tried to run outside.

I got as far as unlocking the door.

In retrospect I may have overreacted a little bit because while I was screaming while running to try and open the door I slipped on the wet tiles and cracked my head against the side of the tub. Not enough to split the skin but just hard enough to whack me unconscious for forty-five minutes.

By then time I came to I was in a robe tucked neatly in my bed with the covers tucked to my chest. Serena came bustling in and when she saw I was awake asked me what I was shrieking about. So I explained.

However her reaction was not what I expected. What I expected was her either telling me I was just dreaming it, though the lump the size of a grapefruit and the horrible pounding in my head disproved that, or that I was nuts. What I really got was her squealing like a school girl with a huge grin splitting her face while squealing 'Yes! Yes! Yes!' over and over again. I sat on the bed, sore, confused and a little worried for Serena's mental health. But that was when she explained everything I knew before attending Abled University.

"You call your mom Serena?" Max asked curiously.

"No. Serena and Troy are... were my parents' best friends and my godparents. My parents died a long time ago"

"Oh..."

Max didn't offer his apology, like most people did, which I was thankful for. I never understood why people, especially people you didn't know, offered their apologies for someone's death. They didn't cause their death nor could they change what happened. I'd rather they stayed quiet.

"So before you found out about your abilities you never even knew about the Abled?" Max asked me with a quizzical eyebrow raised.

"Nope, no idea" I replied popping the 'p'. "When did you find out?"

He smiled slightly and began telling me his story. Apparently it was much different than how I found out. Unlike me, he always knew about the Abled because his parents used their abilities openly around the house. Something I never got to experience.

"When I was little I always watched my parents use their water abilities to float or manoeuvre water around the house. I used to love watching my mom twirl her hands while she washed the dishes and see the water rinse and scrub the dishes my mom held.

"Every day when I would take a bath my parents would play with the tub water. They would twirl their fingers and hands and circle the water around me or make water shapes before making them burst and sprinkle the water over my head" Max smiled as he recalled those childhood memories before continuing, "I would even try to copy the but just end up with a headache because I would forget to breathe"

Max' slight smile disappeared and his eyes unfocused as he continued his story, "One day, when I was eight years old, I was swimming in the lake with my dad like we did almost every day. I remember we were laughing but I don't remember what about when all of a sudden my dad began having convulsions and slumped face first in the water"

He sighed and rubbed a hand through his sandy blonde hair and leaned back onto his elbows, "Now dad was a big fellow, and despite us being in water I couldn't carry him out of the water to the banks. I was so scared. I was screaming for help and rolled dad to his back while I tried to paddle us forward. It didn't really work though, he just kept ducking underwater, not being able to breathe.

"So I did what any eight year old boy would do. I continued to scream... for my mom for anyone to hear me. I started running my hands across the surface of the water" I looked at Max as he continued speaking and saw he was waving his hands across the air showing me what he meant. "I'd seen dad do this before to create waves for me to ride and I guessed this was the only thing I could hope I could do to save his life.

"The in the lake began to roll back and forth like when you sit in a bath tub and sway forwards and backwards and soon a big enough wave pushed us both to the banks. It was a bittersweet moment really, finally being able to use some of my ability, yet when I looked at my dad to celebrate he was still unconscious. I dumped him on his back and he wasn't breathing.

"I started to rub his chest back and forth seeing as I didn't know CPR. I started rubbing in circles on his chest then stroked my hand up towards his throat before blowing air into his mouth and after a few seconds the water started following my actions and spurted out from his mouth and dad started coughing"

It turned out that while Max tried to gather the water in his lungs it was thumping against his heart hard enough to be a weird form of CPR. I was actually really impressed his eight year old self.

"Wow... so you learnt to use your abilities to save your dad" I stated. He just nodded not saying anything. We both fell silent and I tried to imagine what I would do if I had been in his situation. I couldn't even imagine the kind of effects that had on an eight year old boy; the pressure of saving your own dad.

"Helena's been sleeping for ages" Max whined changing the topic completely, "She no fun!"

I smirked and caught his eyes.

I looked out toward the ocean and spread my hands out bringing them together as though I was cupping water and I kept doing this until there was a fairly large amount of water hovering barely above the lapping waves.

"Careful not to let anyone see" Max whispers excitedly.

I winked at him then, when we weren't in danger of having anyone see, I moved the floating water towards us to hover over a sleeping Helena. I thinned it out to blanket over her entire body and with a click of my fingers it all came splashing down.

"Ahhh!" Helena screamed dripping wet. Max and I doubled over in hysterics only to look over at a gaping wet Helena and start all over again. "You guys!" she whined, "Oh ok, I see how it is! Two against one? Well then take this!"

We had no idea what she was talking about until the sand began to shift below us. One second we were laughing and the next we were buried neck deep in the sand.

"Helena no fair!" We yelled in unison, but we were simply met with Helena's hysteric giggles as she sat, sopping wet, under the shade of her umbrella. We managed to wriggle out from the hole and in no time it became a war of sand and water.

"Okay..." Max panted, "How about we promise not to use our abilities for evil on each other?" We all fell back against the soft sand and panted, completely covered in water and sand.

"Agreed." Helena and I agreed at the same time.

"Okay, cleaning time" Helena announced as she sat up. She waved her hands as though she was brushing us down and all the grains of rough sand fell down. I smiled and, as if I was slapping them, I flicked my hand towards the ocean and the beads of water flew across to the sea.

We enjoyed the rest of the day eating the packed food, gulping down drinks and either tanning or swimming. I was currently tanning while I sprawled out on my stomach now that the sun wasn't too strong with the strings of my bikini undone to avoid lines when Max shouted-

"Hey! I thought you didn't want to come?" I just ignored him figuring I didn't know who he was talking to.

"Yeah well, there was nothing else to do" the person replied. My ears perked up. That voice sounded awfully familiar. I racked my brain for the owner of the deep husky voice but couldn't think of the face that matched the voice.

"Well, pull up some sand bro" I felt the sand beside me shift and I turned to greet whoever decided to grace us with their presence when my zeroed on him.

Derrek.

I scowled and rolled my eyes while grunting his presence. It was such a nice day and I had been enjoying myself so much, but it seemed as though today's turn of events had decided I was havin too much of a good time. I turned my head to the other side to ignore him and continued with my tanning.

"Well, someone's crabby today" he sniggered as he tore his shirt off so he was only in his shorts. Just when I start relaxing again I felt a hot finger trail down my spine and I jerked away. I stared incredulously at him narrowing my eyes when he smirked back.

"What do you want?" I snapped at him. He held up a bottle of sun tan lotion and looked pointedly at it then nodded towards his back.

"Can you rub some of this on me?" I continued staring at him. Was he serious? Whether he was serious or not I decided not to humour him.

"No..." I answered, then without another glance I laid my head back down to enjoy the rays of sun. I heard him snigger again.

"That's alright. I don't burn anyway." And I heard him chuckle then shuffled down on the towel.

I was falling in and out of sleep when the sound of Helena and Max laughing in the water woke me up. I felt too hot and thought I might've been out in the sun for too long when I noticed Derrek next to me shoot back to his towel to lay down. Ok...?

I looked over at my two friends in the water then back over to the unattended umbrella and decided that since they weren't using I'd just continue my nap in the shade instead.

It was dark when we finally arrived back at the campus. We hauled all our things back to the room saying goodbye to Max and Derrek. Well, just Max.

"Ugh, I think I might've stayed too long in the sun. I think I got sunburnt" I complained to Helena.

"Ooh, I have the best remedy for that!" She told me and wandered off to one of her many plants. I dumped my bag down and rubbed my shoulders to see her returning with a thick green leaf with little spikes on the side.

"It's aloe vera, it's good for burns" She explained and squeezed the thick leaf. I saw a clear gel ooze out and she collected it with the tips of her fingers. "Take off your top and I'll put some on your back"

I complied and pulled my loose top over my head so I stood in my bikini top and I heard her giggle before slathering on the cooling gel.

"Thanks for that"

"No problem. So... it seems like you and Derrek know each other...?" she said making her statement sound like a question.

"Kind of, I can't stand him though. He's completely arrogant." I replied shaking my head.

"Oh, I wouldn't have guessed." She told me giggling again. I furrowed my eyebrows and wondered how she would have guessed otherwise but let it be.

A little while later I headed to the bathroom to shower when something caught my eye in the mirror. On my left shoulder blade was an obvious sunburn…. saying 'Derrek'.

That ass!

Chapter 5

"**D**errek!" I shouted as I kicked open his door, "Where the hell are you?!"

I looked around the room and saw it was completely void of anyone so I continued to stomp into his and Max's bedroom. Nothing. Where the hell could they both be? It wasn't even fifteen minutes since we left them at the door.

I turned to my left when I heard running water in the bathroom, someone was taking a shower. I wondered who it was. I wasn't sure if the person showering was Max or Derrek, and I didn't want Max to feel the wrath of my revenge. I mean come on, sunburning your name into someone else's skin? Who does that!

I decided that I really didn't care who it was because frankly I just wanted to let some anger loose, and Max would forgive me if it was, in fact, him inside. I closed my eyes and imagined the vapour surrounding me. I held my hand to the door, the tips of my fingers touching the pad of my thumb.

I opened my eyes and spread my fingers wide open against the door. As my fingers spread apart frost seeped out from under my hand and spread across the door making the softest tinkling sound. It encased the door and built up into solid ice around the edges and I imagined it creeping across the walls on the other side.

I could feel the large amount of steam on the other side of the door so I channelled my energy to pick the steam up and slowly freeze it to snow. Now, I concentrated hard on imagining the water droplets cascading down from the shower head and dripping down the body of the person underneath so, with the slightest movements of my fingers, it immediately froze to ice.

"Argh!"

I smiled. My ears were greeted with the shriek of a freezing male which was soon followed by a bang of the shower door, a thud of the man falling on the slippery sleet covered tiles and another banging once he found out the door was frozen shut.

"Valerie!" he shouted.

I coughed out a laugh when I recognised the voice as Derrek's. Thank God for that.

My entertainment was cut short when I saw a faint red glow around the edges of the door and I knew he was melting the ice. I moved to sit on the closest bed as I waited him out, I wasn't going to leave before I could see him half frozen. It only took a few seconds before the melted ice, turned water, was dripping and the door was slammed open by a furious looking Derrek.

Steam poured out of the bathroom disappearing once it mixed with the cooler air and I could see the once frozen bathroom now looked as though it was mildly flooded. Finally my gaze landed on Derrek. He held a soaking wet white towel around his hips and even though he was literally steaming on the spot, his body would shudder every once in a while.

"You are so dead." He gritted out.

"Hey! That was just payback for your stupid prank!" I sneered back half turning and pulling my shirt down my shoulder to show his name blazing on my shoulder blade.

He smirked and pulled the towel tighter around him.

"Suits you."

I gaped at him. That's it?

"That's all you have to say?!"

"Yep" he replied before strutting to the wardrobe. He turned his head so he was looking over his shoulder and asked, "Now if you don't mind I'd like to change"

Instantly he dropped his towel and I only just managed to spin around squeezing my eyes shut. Blood flushed my cheeks and I scurried out of there. At least he didn't see me blushing.

"I can feel the heat from your cheeks all the way from here!" He yelled as I reached for the door.

Damnit.

History.

Water skills.

Combat.

Abilities Tutorial.

Biology.

I read my schedule again and chuckled when biology was the only normal subject in my itinerary that taught the same things as a non-Abled subject. Last week was apparently an 'introduction' for all the Abled because many hadn't even known what the Abled were, which was a relief for me. At least I wasn't the only one.

I headed to history with Helena in tow and found our seats again. The room was buzzing with light chatter and the odd laughter when Mr Arbit entered with a bang of the door. I guessed this was his usual entrance for class.

"Welcome class, welcome, welcome, welcome once again!" he sang out with a smile. "Now who here read the rest of The Stinger Eradication?"

A show of hands were raised but he chuckled when the majority obviously didn't bother but when they fell back down and one hand remained up Mr Arbit pointed to the student in question.

"Yes? You have a question?" he called out.

"Yes, I do. I did the reading you gave us but there was something that I was a little confused about." The student was a lanky boy with shoulder length curly blonde hair and light freckles splotched across his nose and cheeks.

"Oh? Well do go on then" Mr Arbit encouraged him.

"Well, the reading said that all Stingers were annihilated all around the world but how does The Control know that? I heard that there was a group of Stingers that were able to flee before being sought out and that now they're in hiding somewhere." The lanky boy explained. "No one knows where, but I heard that the Stingers wanted revenge and would take it out on the rest of the Abled community!"

I raised an eyebrow at him. He seemed like one of those people who would believe every single thing they heard and stand on a soap box shouting out the world will end soon. Apparently Mr Arbit thought he same.

"Indeed. Mr...?"

"Colin Terra"

"Mr Terra. Well I've heard that as well and I can assure you that that is purely a rumour to scare the community. Both Stingers and Healers are telepathic and therefore The Control would have used the telepathy of the Healers to find the Stingers in hiding." Mr Arbit argued.

That silenced Colin and after his outburst the class continued.

"Well that was... yeah I got nothing" Max yawned as Helena and I left history. "Do you have water skills next Val?"

"Sure do. We'll catch you later Helena" I said as Max and I veered towards our next class.

"So... I heard what you did to Derrek..." Max said trying to hide a grin.

"And...?"

"Nothing, nothing. I was just wondering what would make you do that, not that it wasn't funny"

I rolled my eyes but showed him the 'Derrek' sunburn. He howled with laughter not even a second later and I quickly covered my shoulder mumbling about how immature guys can be. I walked faster leaving Max behind.

"Wai-wait Val! I'm sorry! It's just... you have to admit, it is pretty funny" he breathed trying not to laugh. It wasn't working.

"No, it's not Max. This will take forever to go away!"

"I'm sorry, sorry!" I just rolled my eyes and changed the topic while we continued walking.

We walked into a huge white tiled room with a large circular pool of water in the middle. This class was supposed to be specifically for the Water-abled to help them advance and improve their abilities. I was actually really excited about this class, I wanted to learn as much as I could about my mother and my ability.

"Good morning class" a wistful woman's voice announced.

Everyone turned but couldn't see who spoke. It seemed as though she was right in front of us but there wasn't anyone there. She chuckled. I looked around for the invisible lady and I noticed the water of the pool ripples slightly. Suddenly the water in the pool spurted upwards into a fountain. Everyone gasped then 'oohed' and 'ahhed' as the fountain took shape of a slim woman.

She opened her midnight blue almond shaped eyes, and then her smile appeared. Slowly another feature appeared one after the other until finally her skin transformed from the flowing water to a glowing milky white. Her long raven hair was parted down the middle and she wore a long one shouldered blue dress that was imprinted with the ripples of the water.

That was amazing! The class erupted in excited chatter and applause and the teacher simply smiled at us until we quietened before she stepped onto the tiled surface.

"The Water-abled. Uncontrollable and mysterious like the ocean. We are the life source of all natural beings and in time, you will be able to do as I did just moments before. My name is Ms Flumine and I am your teacher for water skills" Ms Flumine stated. She had a soft voice that was laced with a strong underlying tone.

We were separated into pairs and were asked to do simple tasks such as raise the water from the pool or make shapes or freeze the water. It was an introductory class where Ms Flumine found out what we could or couldn't do as well as our strengths and weaknesses. It was a fun class!

"Well, Valerie you really are your mother's daughter" she murmured as I executed a more difficult task.

The bubbling fountain of water I was standing on collapsed as I took in what she said and I screamed as I fell into the pool. "What do you mean? Did you know my mom?" I gasped as I coughed up water.

"Indeed I did my dear" she didn't elaborate and just as I was about to ask more she spoke loudly to the class, "Well it seems as though class has come to an end for now. I will see you all next time."

I barely had time to hop out of the pool, dripping wet, before she spun around swiftly turning herself to water and flying into the depths of the pool. "Do you think she just stays there? Or she does that until we leave?" Max asked as he came up behind me.

"I have no idea" I replied distractedly as I gathered all the water from my drenched clothes and threw it back into the pool and once I was completely dry again we left. I was distracted by what she said about my mother. I'd have to ask her more about my mother when I find the time, or even just find her.

I had a spare two hours before I had my combat class so I decided to grab something to eat and maybe change into something more comfortable to whatever will happen in combat.

I was running late. Oh God I hope the combat coach wasn't one of those cliché drill sergeants that shouted until spit came flying into your face. No such luck. I burst through the doors of an auditorium it seemed, though it was much different to the ones in high school. It was massive, absolutely colossal and had sections that were obviously in favour to each Abled.

There was a forest that lurked in the corner with tall trees strangled with vines and other such plants. A desert with craters and mounds of dirt that spurted fire every so often as though it was cut out straight from the Jurassic ages. Across from it was a lake of deep dark water surrounded by smooth grey rocks and rock pools. Finally there was a simple off-white tiled area with several hospital style beds and chairs.

"You're late!"

The shout startled me out from gazing around the auditorium and I rushed over the rest of the class who were, like myself, clad in either short or tights and a comfortable singlet or t-shirt with sneakers.

"I'm so sorry sir, I got lost" I stammered to the hulk-like man with shoulder length brown hair. He was bulging with muscles that were straining against his clothing. The class laughed softly at my exclamation and I wondered why.

The hulk turned to look straight at me and I could see why. Hulk was in fact a she-hulk. Oops.

"Fine. Join the rest of the class." She-hulk snapped. "As I was saying, this class is about being able to use your abilities for offense and defence situations as well as strengthening your mind and body. Now, I will set you up with partners of a different ability then" she paused with an evil smirk, "you take one team down at a time.'

"Rules! No life threatening manoeuvres. Our newbie healers are on hand but they are not up to life threatening healing just yet. Let me repeat that you are to take other teams out... not kill them. Now as I call your name pair up!"

She began calling off names and I can only hope to get Helena since Max and I are both Water-abled. I looked around and saw Derrek leaning against a tree with his leg crossed the other snapping his fingers making fire appear and disappear like a lighter.

"Max and Derrek" She-hulk called.

"Valerie and Colin" I stood up and sighed as I saw lanky Colin offer me a shy wave and stood by me. She-hulk finished off the names and I noticed Helena was paired with another pretty girl.

"Now, if you take out a team and they are unable to signal the healers or myself you are to signal us with your ability by shooting something up in the air. Any questions? No? Ok, well call out to me if anything life threatening occurs."

Colin's hand crept up.

"Yes?"

"Uh, what exactly do we call you? You never told us your name..."

The coach glared at him and snapped, "My name is Coach Shulk"

I choked loudly as I tried on my life to not burst into laughter. Coach Shulk? God, I was closer than I thought when I was calling her she-hulk. Colin gave me a few hard slaps to the back, which were harder than I could give him credit for, and Coach Shulk rolled her eyes.

"Try not to die just yet Miss Cascade" Coach Shulk called out before turning away.

"Healers, by the infirmary" she called out and several students stepped over to the tiled area. "Now go!"

The shrill of a whistle echoed around the auditorium and every couple raced around. I didn't know what Colin's ability was but I just followed him to the forest. As we ran I tried to glance around at where the most couples ran off to and it seemed like the forest was a popular spot. More hiding spots I supposed.

We ran to a secluded spot that was heading downhill and crouched down by a huge twisting tree. "So what's your ability?" I whispered, keeping an eye out for other people.

"Earth. You?"

"Water"

"Nice. We should be fine together then. So what did you want to do? Wait or go on the offensive?" Colin spoke with such authority which was much different to the shy geeky guy he portrayed earlier.

"How about we wait a bit then run on the offensive?" He nodded his head once and we settled ourselves into more comfortable crouches as we waited for passing couples. We waited merely two minutes before a couple came running through.

"You take the guy on the left and I'll take the right" Colin whispered. I nodded once to confirm.

I gathered the molecules from the leaves above the guy and when he was in position the water came gushing down on top of him. As it splashed down over his body I spread my fingers apart and the water froze encasing the guy inside.

A cry of another guy caught my attention and for a moment I thought Colin had been caught. As I leapt over a fallen tree trunk the sight before me caught me by surprise. Colin was walking towards me with a smile and the guy he took on looked as though he was growing from a large boulder that reached above his elbows.

"Wow, awesome job Colin" I praised him raising my hand for a hi-5. He slapped his hand against mine. To signal the coach Colin shot a large wad of dirt into the air high above the tree tops and I shot a stream of water through it causing it to burst like a muddy firework.

"Ok students we have two couples left. Let's go!" Coach Shulk's voice boomed over the loud speaker.

Colin and I were exhausted. We were filthy and muddy and quite frankly I was getting sick of the forest. We'd managed to take down ten couples just by staying in the forest and since there was one couple left I thought it was safe to say that they wouldn't be stupid enough to stroll in here.

I voiced my opinion to Colin and he agreed resulting in us protecting each other's backs as we crept towards the lake. We decided it would be our best shot there seeing as there were both water and rocks and Colin had already shown his strengths with shifting rocks and dirt instead of plants like Helena.

"Coast is clear... let's go!" He whispered and we made a wild dash for a particularly rocky area right next the lake.

He ran first, crouching and running until he made it to the larger boulders. He turned to me and his eyes widened to the size of plates.

"Valerie! Look out!" he shouted. I turned to look behind me and saw a huge flaming ball of fire throttling towards me. I didn't have enough time to scream so instead I followed my instincts and I grabbed the water from the lake and threw it across my body.

The fireball collided against of my water encased body and I could practically feel the sizzle of the flames as it died. I saw from the corner of my eye Derrek's surprised face. Behind him Max slapped the back of his head but Derrek ignored him and caught the flames that were thrown up by the mounds of dirt in the desert area.

I let the water thicken around me and turned to Colin.

"Colin, I'll take Derrek. You take Max, do not underestimate him!" Before he could reply I felt another sizzle of a dying fireball at my back.

"My turn" I whispered to myself.

I bent my knees and spread my arms wide imagining the entire lake as I attempted to lift it up. I could feel the weight of the water straining my body but I ignored it. Derrek thinks he can just fire while my back's turned? I don't think so. That was the cheapest shot!

Moving the large amount of water was slower because of the sheer weight of it but as I gathered it all and shift my body to ready myself to attack I felt fireball after fireball sizzling against my head, back and legs but nothing could penetrate my water shield.

Suddenly I threw all my body weight around to face Derrek with my arms following my movement and the next I saw was Derrek as he crossed his arms in an 'X' to shield himself. A tidal wave of murky water beat down on him and it was too much for a Fire-abled.

He collapsed under it and, by the look of it, was unconscious.

"Holy sh*t" Colin murmured as he leaned on my shoulder with his elbow. "You are one psycho chick. I will never mess with you. Ever."

I chuckled and turned to face him. "Where's Max?"

He smiled and nodded his head to the right. I followed his direction and found Max dangling on the edge of the forest in the air by vines the size of pythons. An applause erupted and I realised the class had been watching us.

"Great job Cascade and Terra" Coach Shulk boomed as she slapped us on the back. Class was dismissed and it seemed that since it went overtime that Abilities Tutorial and Biology were postponed until next time. Thank God! I hadn't had a work out like that in too long.

"Great job Valerie. We make a great team" Colin said with a kind smile. His shirt was ripped and hanging off of him in near tatters but what shocked me was that he wasn't the lanky guy I thought him to be.

His strength with his earth abilities were to do with rocks and earth, pretty much the non-living things and with having to manipulate such heavy materials he was quite in shape. He was tall and thin but it was the washboard abs that threw me off.

"Call me Val, and yeah we did make quite the team"

We chatted as we walked towards our rooms and I found out he was also living on the same floor and was room number 401.

"I'll see you around, Val" he waved and closed the door behind him. I continued on to my room seeing nothing but the polished wooden floors and plain walls but stopped dead when I saw a large dark figure leaning against my door.

Derrek.

"What are you doing here Derrek?" I groaned as I tried to bypass him.

He flipped me swiftly so that I was now the one against the door and he caged me in with his strong arms. He leaned in so close I could smell the woody smell emanating from him until our noses nearly touched.

"Listen closely Tadpole, you ever show me up like that again and I will make you pay. No one makes me look weak" he growled softly staring straight into my eyes.

I was almost hypnotised. His eyes penetrated into me and I felt like I was losing my breath. My fingertips tingled and I could feel it spreading up my fingers to my hands and arms. I shook my head and glared back at him.

"Don't you ever threaten me Sparky, if I made you look weak then I guess our conclusion is that you are, in fact, weak. Get over yourself."

With those parting words I shoved him away and quickly unlocked the door slamming it hard behind me as I managed to escape his hypnotising presence.

Chapter 6

I slammed the door shut in his face and leaned against it blowing out a deep breath. What the hell was that? I could still feel the weird tingling in my hands and fingers from when we were almost touching. It was like little pin pricks but felt... nice. Pain and pleasure at the same time.

I shook my head. Get yourself together woman!

I shoved off the door and walked towards the balcony. Was it really just over a week that Derrek had shown a kind side only to hide it beneath this harsh exterior? Who was he? It didn't matter I guessed since neither one of us were interested in the other.

I grasped the cool metal of the railing from the balcony and stared at the view. Below me were the grassy grounds where students lounged about chatting and reading. A group further off played a game of Frisbee.

Further away stood the forest where I'd bumped into Derrek doing whatever the hell he was doing. It was a large forest and the trees packed closer together the farther along you looked. Beside it stood a large sparkling lake that reflected the setting sun and the birds that flew overhead.

I sighed. I missed Serena and Troy. Troy's father figure personality that, at this time, would tell me any boy wouldn't be good enough for me and not to let it get to me then Serena's teenage attitude that would be poking and prodding me for juicy gossip and details.

I smiled at the memory of them.

"Hey chicky" Helena called as she entered the room, "You were a-ma-zing in combat!"

"Thanks, I didn't even see you and your partner the whole time"

"Yeah, we got taken out pretty easily because she was Water-abled but wasn't particularly good and I don't like violence" she shrugged before flopping onto the sofa. We continued chatting away into the night only pausing to order Chinese food and change into comfy sweats and tank top for me and a loose night shirt and shorts for her.

"So... what's the deal with you and Derrek?" she asked me tilting her head in curiosity as she munched on her fried rice.

"Honestly, I have no idea. He's got worse mood swings than a girl! He was really nice to me on my birthday but I haven't seen that considerate guy ever since. I'm just going to ignore him" I answered her, and truth be told, my words were going to be a lot harder to follow than anticipated.

Helena and I continued talking throughout the night until she passed out on her bed. I yawned and soon followed after her.

The air was dank and my nose twitched at the rancid smell emanating around me. Where was I? It was dark except for the odd melting wax candle situated on the rocks protruding from the walls. From what I could see, which wasn't much, I was trapped in some cavern. The roof was a mixture of moist dirt and hard rock. "Hello?" I called out to the darkness. My greeting echoed around me sending chills down my spine. "Is anyone there?"

Again, my voice ricocheted off the walls.

I slowly took steps forward, squinting my eyes to try and find a passage or an exit somewhere. I was rewarded with a narrow tunnel. Should I follow it, I wondered. It was my best option. I dragged my hands across the grimy walls to help me walk forward ignoring the moist moss growing there. As I walked into the larger chamber I sighed in relief when the smell was a bit weaker. There were more candles lit in this chamber and they flickered around the many dark passages that connected to this one.

"Hello?" I shouted once again, even though I already knew no one would answer besides my echoes.

"Good evening Valerie" I jumped as my voice stuck in my throat at the unexpected reply.

"Wh-who's there? Where am I?" I cried out.

"Tut, tut, tut Valerie. Now is not the time for questions" the voice replied. The voice was a deep growl of a man who spoke as though he had all the time in the world. He was dangerous. Even without knowing who he was or what he looked like, I could sense that he was not someone to mess with.

"Where are you!" I shouted, tired of his games. I was not in the mood to be toyed with.

A malicious chuckle broke out, multiplying the echoes down the tunnels and a large hooded figure stepped out from a shadowed corner. He was tall with a dark maroon cloak with a hood that obscured all his face besides his evil smirk. Only his pale white hands peaked out from the folds of his disguise.

"What do you want?" I gasped in terror stepping backwards to somehow escape his hidden stare.

"Why dear Valerie... I want you" he answered with a smile displaying his yellowing pointed teeth.

Then he clawed forward at my throat.

I screamed.

I screamed and screamed and thrashed around unable to move my bounded legs.

"Val! Valerie! Wake up!"

Someone was slapping my face and I woke with a start gasping beautiful fresh air. Helena was sitting on my bed hugging me tight and whispering that everything was alright, that I was safe and I was only having a nightmare.

"It was just a nightmare... just a nightmare sweety. Shh..." she rocked me back and forth like a mother consoling her scared child.

I was crying now and my breath hitched with every intake. It took another half hour of Helena consoling me before my sobs ceased. My throat felt raw and my nose was blocked but I was feeling a lot better.

"Thanks Helena. I'm so sorry you had to see me like that." I sniffed. "I'll be okay, you can go back to sleep"

She looked at me warily for a few seconds before asking if I was sure. I nodded and offered her a slight smile before she gave me another tight hug and slipped back into her bed.

I sighed. There was no way in hell I was going back to sleep tonight.

The next day were the classes we missed out on yesterday so I was able to down a few cups of coffee to wake myself up before heading off to Abilities Tutorial. There was a select few students here instead of the large amounts of people I was used to and I pulled a face when both Max and Helena weren't in this class.

Derrek was though. Great...

The room was similar to the classrooms in high school so I plonked myself down on the back corner desk and began doodling on my notebook again. I heard the legs of the chair beside me scrape against the floor and the woody smell of the person enveloped me.

I glanced at my neighbour and slumped in my seat.

"What are you doing?" I sneered at Derrek. I really wasn't in the mood for his antics.

" Sitting" he grumbled back.

"Whatever. Just don't bug me"

"Good afternoon class! I'm sorry I'm late woah-!" A short lady that I'm assuming was our teacher bustled into the classroom and tripped over her feet tumbling onto the ground sending papers flying into the air.

Oh my God! I stood up to help her but the girls in front of the class were already helping her up.

"Oh my… thank you my dears" she said popping her extra large glasses back on. Her glasses magnified her eyes and her think lips curved into a kind smile.

She kind of looked like a hippy with big blonde-grey hair held back with a scarf and layers of thin baggy gypsy tops floating over black leggings and sandals. The girls who helped her up sat back to their seats and we all stared at the teacher.

"Um, uh yes. My name is Ms Insolita and I'm teaching you all about your abilities" she stammered. The class droned on as Ms Insolita rambled about how each of our abilities worked. She spoke like a frightened child and her eyes darted side to side as though she was about to flee. I looked up at Derrek but he was facing the front with his elbow propped up on the desk and his hand supporting his chin.

I was dead tired. Exhausted.

Everytime I closed my eyes the hooded man's skeletal fingers reached for me and I'd jump, scaring myself awake. I knew it was just a nightmare but it felt so real. On top of being exhausted, my head pounded like a jackhammer was going loose across my brain and I just wanted to get out of here.

"Hey, you ok Tadpole?" Derrek cocked his head to the side and waited for me to answer.

"I'm fine. Why do you care Sparky?" I grumbled back rubbing my hands over my face.

"I don't" then with that parting phrase he stood up and left making me realise that class was over without me noticing.

Derrek's POV

I had a pounding headache.

I walked through the campus towards my next class, biology, and the flood of students parted like the red sea to let me pass. Usually I'd smirk but last night exhausted me. I'd had the same dream last night but it was different. Last night I dreamt that Val was in my place and I watched from above like a bat secured by its wings. I don't know why I'd dream about her but I can only think that last night I was lucky not to be in her place.

In abilities tutorial I couldn't help but sense Val was troubled. As soon I stepped into the class frustration and exhaustion flew at me from her direction and I couldn't help sitting next to her. I wanted to ignore her and pretend she didn't exist because there was something about her that made me feel the need to be cautious.

I turned into biology and slumped into my seat. "Hey man, you look like crap"

I turned my head and saw Max grinning at me. "Yeah well, you always look like crap" I countered lamely.

"Wait, wasn't Val in your class?" he asked looking around me to see if she was coming.

"Yeah and...?"

"Well, shouldn't she be here by now?"

"Seriously Max, what's so good about her? You've known her for as long as I have and you're sounding like a whining possessive boyfriend"

He looked dejected at his notebook. "Yeah, I know. But I just feel like she and I connect somehow"

I rolled my eyes. Max was that cliché romantic pretty boy and whenever he talked like this I zoned out. Class started when a tall dark man walked swiftly into the lecture theatre in a suit and ordered us to be quiet.

"Quiet please, we have a lot to go through today. I am Professor Pulcher, yes it is latin for 'handsome' and I will not disagree with it" he began. I chuckled at his straight forward joke but wondered if it really was latin. "Now everyone turn to page three hundred and fifty-"

"Do you think she's ok?" Max whispered to me.

I looked over at Max and raised an eyebrow, completely oblivious to what he going on about "Who?"

"Val! She's not here..." I looked around and saw he was right, not that I really cared. I closed my eyes and focused on her thoughts.

"She's fine" I told Max trying not to fall asleep in class.

"But how do you know-"

"I just do, now shut up" I grunted firmly.

Chapter 7

I jerked awake, sweat beading down my forehead and dampening my clothes.

Every night ever since that first nightmare I'd been having the same dream over and over again. I do the same thing and yet it scares me just as much as the first time and every time I wake up I have a throbbing headache. It's been weeks! Months!

Thank God we had a week off to 'study' before our exams and I'd decided to pay a visit to Troy and Serena. Familiar faces and a home cooked meal is what I needed for sure. I started packing and glanced outside, the sun was barely rising and the morning birds had just woken up singing good morning songs for their chicks.

I finished packing in a matter of minutes and looked over at a sleeping Helena. She'd been worried about me and took the role of mother trying to force me to eat 'a little something' or talk to her about it. But I didn't want to. It just felt like this nightmare was something personal and I just couldn't find it in myself to tell her, or anyone. I didn't want to wake her so I changed into short gym shorts and a tank top then tied my hair up in a high ponytail before slipping on my running shoes.

This had been my routine lately. Waking up freaked out of my mind, wash my face, change, go running. I never knew how long I'd run for but the sun would be shining brightly and some days I'd end up being late for my morning classes.

I walked outside and began stretching my limbs warming them up and breathing the fresh morning air. The grass was wet with dew drops and the crushed blades of grass stuck to the soles of my sneakers. I began running. The feel of the chilly air breezed past my face and made me feel fresh and safe.

I started running laps around the campus and on my fifth lap I turned for the lake. I felt much more at ease around the water. The lake was my element. It was huge so I ran around and around feeling the lake water swivel and stir like it was magnetised to me. I ran until the sun blazed down on me and my muscles ached with over use.

I pushed myself farther and harder and enjoyed the feel of my core temperature rising and sweat cooling my skin then finally I collapsed on the bank of the lake. I breathed hard and worked to get my heart rate to slow down as well as my breathing. Most students would be inside their rooms or the library studying hard but I wouldn't have been able to concentrate hard enough to do that.

I tugged my shoes and socks off and dipped my heated feet into the cool lake water. I sighed as a smile tugged at my lips, it felt so refreshing I cupped the water with my hands and splashed my face. It wasn't enough so I thought, 'oh why not?'

I tore my top and shorts off leaving me in my bra and panties before diving into the cold liquid. The water rejuvenated my body as I swam. I swam deep and far and loved how the world could be forgotten as long as I was underwater. I reached the bottom of the lake and looked around at the underwater marine life.

Slippery rocks with plants growing on and in between them varying in shades of green. Little fish of pinks, green, blues and yellows darted through the swaying plants and schools of them rushed past me. Marine life weren't scared of me, as a Water-abled I comfortably fit in amongst them.

I planted my feet on the soft bottom of the lake and pushed up kicking for the surface. All too soon I decided I should get going if I wanted to make it home before nightfall. I pulled myself out of the lake and froze when I saw a half naked Derrek sitting by my pile of clothes. He wore basketball shorts and sneakers with earphones dangling around his neck. He smirked when he saw me and his eyes roamed down my body.

"I thought you might have drowned for a minute there Tadpole" he called to me.

"You wish Sparky" I replied snippily as I ignored his heated looks and stepped over to him. I went to grab my clothes but he snatched them away and stood up. "Hey!" I yelled, "Give them back!"

"I don't know... what are you willing to give me in exchange?" he asked twirling my shorts around in the air with his finger.

"A punch to the face or a kick in the nuts... your choice assface" I gritted clenching my fists.

"Hmm, neither. I think I'll just keep them" then he began jogging away. Aw crap I didn't think of that.

"Hey come back! Give me back my clothes you piece of sh-"

"Uh, uh, uh watch your language there Tadpole" he interrupted me. I ran after him only feeling half self-conscious at my near nakedness. I caught up to him at the edge of the forest and tackled him to the ground.

"I said give me back my clothes!" I screamed at him. I straddled him and began punching his chest while trying to grab my clothes but he had an annoying long sexy torso and he kept it out of my reach.

"Damn Tadpole if you wanted me on my back you could've said so" he laughed as he held my clothes higher above head and gripped my waist with the other to prevent me from sliding up.

"Shut up you jerk, I just want my clothes!" He stood up and I fell backwards landing on my ass and before I could stop him my clothes had spouts of purple fire dancing along them.

"What the hell are you doing?!" I screamed. I collected the water that still clung to me and threw it at my clothes making sure he was splashed as well and grabbed them. I checked them over and growled. He had purposely burnt two holes in my tank top in the chest area and two holes in the back of my shorts.

"You're such an ass Derrek" I growled before throwing on my clothes anyway and stomping away.

"Nice ass Tadpole!" he shouted after me with laughter. I stomped back to snatch my shoes with my socks hidden inside and marched back up to the university. Despite having thrown all the water from my body I still shivered slightly and my skin was cool to the touch.

"Uh... what in the world happened to you Val?" Helena asked when I strode in slamming the front door.

"I'll give you one guess..." I murmured.

"Whoa! Not that I'm complaining about the view but what happened to you?!" Max cried as he strode in from the kitchen.

"Derrek" Helena answered him for me.

Max's eyebrows furrowed as he registered her answer. "Derrek? Why? I didn't know you hung out with him Val, I thought you hated the guy?"

"I do... I went for a run this morning then a swim and when I left the lake Sparky himself was there with my clothes then took off... long story short, I may have pissed him off"

"Sparky?"

"Derrek"

"You call him Sparky?" Max was being very curious today. I looked up at him leaning his hip against the kitchen bench and sighed.

"Yeah I guess, just like he calls me Tadpole. It just kind of stuck I suppose" I shrugged my shoulders. Max nodded and mumbled something before excusing himself to study.

"What did he say? What the hell was that about?" I asked Helena who just smiled.

"He said 'I don't get a nick name'" she replied then giggled before dancing off to talk to her plants again.

O-kay?

I didn't have time to ponder what was causing Max to act like a sulking baby so I stepped into the bathroom to shower and waved goodbye to Helena as I took off to visit home.

"Valerie!" Serena shrieked when I walked into the house. I was engulfed in a tight hug and I laughed hugging her just as tightly back. It was a good thing I had Helena otherwise Serena's personality might have overwhelmed me.

Troy was working late so Serena and I ordered pizza for dinner and watched chick flicks while catching up. I'd always loved being home. It wasn't a gigantic house, it was cozy and painted with warm whites, creams and browns. We sat on the soft sofa each holding a slice of pizza while watching Mean Girls when I decided to tell Serena about my dream.

"-and it happens every night! I wake up with the worst headache as if something was crawling all over my brain. It... it scares me to sleep" I finished off quietly. Serena had stayed silent throughout my spiel nodding her head to indicate she was listening intently.

"I don't like it." She said gravely. "The feeling you're having, the headaches, you said it feels like something's crawling on your brain?"

"Yeah, but I didn't literally mean that something was-"

"No, no I know I'm just making sure" she cut me off. She stayed silent but had a look of concentration on her face which turned to indecision. She sighed and rubbed her hands over her face and for once she didn't seem like the bouncy young at heart Serena I'd always known. She looked like she aged ten years with tiredness lining her face and like the wise woman I knew her to be.

"I think we need to have a serious talk Val" she said.

I'd never seen her so serious before and it freaked me out a little bit.

"Okay, shoot" I replied curiously.

"As you know, your mother, Karissa, and I were best friends. Both of us were Water-abled and back when we were younger everyone only befriended an Abled of the same ability. It was like an unspoken rule." She started and as she continued her story I felt myself imagining myself in her position.

"Abled University housed all abilities, including the now extinct Stingers. Stingers weren't common, they were actually quite rare but what with most Abled attending Abled University there was a group of Stingers that walked the halls together. They were like the greasers of the Abled community"

Serena's flashback

"Oh God there he is again" Karissa sighed biting her lip. I followed her gaze and sighed as well, but not with admiration. She twirled her long wavy blonde hair around her slender finger and her jade green eyes were glued to him.

"Karissa what are you doing? You can't just swoon after him!" I whisper yelled at her grabbing her elbow and pulling us both around the corner to stop her ogling.

"I can't help it! He's just so... so raw. He's like the ultimate bad boy!" she gushed.

She had the look of a love struck woman with stars in her eyes and I knew she was a goner. I'd spent the last two years keeping her away from him and keeping her crush a secret from the world. Brad Cascade. Leader of the Stinger group and even I would admit he was a catch.

He had olive skin held taut over his muscles and lean body with dark brown hair and blue eyes. His devilish smile showed off his sparkling white teeth and I could see why my best friend had eyes only for him. Not only was he good looking but he was total forbidden fruit.

Just then Brad himself strutted around the corner and I noticed that he and Karissa's eyes caught each other and lingered for just a second too long. Oh no, that can't be good.

End of flashback – Valerie's POV

Ho-ly crap!

"My dad was a Stinger!" I screamed at Serena. She flinched at my high pitched scream but recovered then nodded slow-ly.

"Yes honey he was. But I am telling you now that he never used his pain ability! He was half Stinger and half Healer to be exact. He only ever used telepathy and he was a good man. A wonderful husband to your mother and a terrific father to you" she added sadly.

I was shell shocked as her little bit of held back information dropped on me like a nuclear bomb. I can't believe after all this time no one ever told me. I knew what I had been thinking when I first heard about The Stinger Eradication was true. My father was a Stinger – a… good Stinger?

Then I closed my eyes, squeezing them shut as I asked the most crucial question that had affected my life, "How did my parents really die?"

At the age of two I wouldn't have remembered anything.

Not the crash of the door as the Abled army came smashing through the entrance and breaking everything in sight. Not the screams of my mother as she cried salty tears and hid me in the back of the closet with her final kiss to my forehead, nor the shouting of my father and the agonizing cries of pain that filtered through the sunshine yellow cottage.

I wouldn't have remembered anything.

What I do remember were the flickering images of dust motes that spiralled down from the woollen blankets that were folded away until next winter that caused me to feel drowsy and fall asleep. Apparently Brad, my father, sent a mental message to Serena explaining what happened and to take care of me from now on. Apparently my parents' last words were cries of love for me.

But I didn't remember anything.

I laid on my back on my bed staring at the ceiling fan spin its circuit over and over again wondering about my parents. My mother saved my life. My father sacrificed himself to save my mother even though she shouldn't have been murdered anyway.

Mom was Water-abled. Dad was a Stinger.

I didn't realise how fortunate I was to have inherited my mother's ability and not my dad's. I couldn't imagine what I would be like had I been a Stinger with the abilities to inflict pain in a blink of an eye. I wish I did though. I wish I could've had that ability and torture every single pathetic piece of trash that murdered my parents.

A knock on the door jolted me out of my gory day dreams and Serena crept in with two mugs of steaming tea. "You okay darling?" she asked me quietly blowing the steam rising from her tea.

"Fine" I replied robotically. We sipped on our tea in silence. "I have a question"

"Yes?"

"When I explained how it felt after I had my nightmare, how it was like something crawling on my brain or something, you said you didn't like it. Like you 'd heard something about it before?" I asked leaving the question hanging in the air.

She sighed and nodded. "Yes I've heard about it... experienced it..."

"Really?" I leaned forward very intrigued at her answer.

"Like you said it feels like something is crawling on your brain. It's as though you can't control the images or words running through your own head and sometimes you're aware of your surroundings but more than likely you're forced to live out whatever is being forced on you"

I nodded. That's exactly what it felt like. It was horrible and painful and sent shivers down my spine. "Yes, that's exactly right. What is it Serena?"

She paused, flinching at the memory of having her mind overtaken. "It's the feeling of when a Stinger uses his telepathy on you"

I froze. No, she must be wrong.

"You must be mistaken Serena. All Stingers were destroyed in The Stinger Eradication, I read about it and heard about it in history at university. Maybe it was a Healer or something? They have telepathy too"

She shook her head, her facial expression grave.

"No sweetheart, when Healers use telepathy on someone it has a calming and peaceful effect. Healers are all positive energy, the complete opposite of Stingers. Healers will not and cannot make anyone feel like that"

"But... what does that mean?" I asked in a low voice.

Chapter 8

How ironic was this visit home...?

I came home with the intention of relaxing and getting over this paranoia from the nightmare. Every night I'd have that same nightmare and every night I'd woken up in sweats wishing I'd never gone to sleep. Now here I am, safe in the security of home with my favourite people in the world when this ridiculous bomb of information slaps me in the face!

My dad was a Stinger.

My dad and mom were murdered.

I'm half Stinger.

There's another Stinger somewhere out there who was forcing themselves into my head as I slept.

I shivered. That was the creepy part. It was almost like mind rape with no way to escape. I got flashes of Nightmare on Elm Street and realised this was almost the same. There was no escaping it. I mentally slapped myself, now here I was thinking my life was a horror movie!

The ding of a timer softly broke me out of my deep thoughts and I slipped on a pair of floral oven mitts to take out the soft triple chocolate cookies I'd been baking. With the mountain of issues I'd been going through lately I desperately was in need of a chocolate fix, plus baking helped take my mind off things. Well it used to.

I inhaled the warm, sickly sweet aroma of fresh cookies and quickly pinched one off the baking tray. Good God that was insanely hot! Why did I not think of that?! I threw it from one hand to the other letting it cool off while I juggled the delicious treat.

When it was just cool enough to hold without scalding my fingers I took a bite. My pearly teeth easily bit through the soft cookie and every chocolate chip melted in my mouth. Now this, this was what I needed. I baked another two trays of cookies before I sat on the bench stool and one after the other.

"Hey shrimp, it's great to see you" Troy greeted me as he walked into the kitchen. He stole the unbitten cookie I was holding and took a bite.

"Hey Troy, I'm ok. How was work?" Troy was a fire fighter, which was one of the many reasons why Serena fell for him, and due to that he always smelt faintly of ash.

"It's ok. Slow, but that's always a good thing" he replied with a half shrug. He joined me by the bench and ate cookies with me while we spoke about generic topics.

"So... Serena told me she told you the truth" Troy said nonchalantly staring at the wall.

"Yep" I replied popping the last bite of my cookie into my mouth. I didn't need to ask what he was talking about. It was pretty obvious.

"I'm sorry Val, if you ever need someone to talk to, you know I'm always there for you" Troy voiced patting my shoulder. I nodded. And that was all we spoke about it. Troy didn't dig into what I was thinking, how I was taking it, what I wanted to do about it because he knew me... and he knew I wouldn't want to talk about it.

"Val honey did you want the rest of the cookies you baked?" Serena called out to me from the kitchen.

"Sure" I called back. I was packing my things again getting ready to go back to university. I didn't get the completely relaxed time I wanted to achieve here but I'll be damned if I go back without some cookies!

"Thanks for dropping by honey. Come back whenever you want ok?" Serena encouraged while Troy nodded. I hugged them both and brought the roof of my convertible down before waving and driving off towards university.

I worshipped the feeling of the cool wind rushing past. It flipped my blonde hair around making it whip against my face but I didn't care. It felt freeing and I stepped on the gas to feel the rush even more. The sun beamed down from the cloudless sky and I couldn't help but think today was such a beautiful day.

Suddenly a golden streak caught my attention at the last second as it appeared in front of my speeding car. I immediately stomped my foot on the break and swung the steering wheel around in hopes of missing the mysterious animal.

The screeching of my tyres pierced my ears as the rubber ground against the gravel underneath. When I finally pulled to a stop I let out the breath I didn't know I was holding out as pried my white fingers from the leather of my steering wheel. Thank God I was the only car on the road for ages!

"What the hell was that?" I gasped to myself looking side to side for whatever the golden thing was. A light gold patch caught my eye in the trees by the road and I popped the door open and slid a leg out as I went to investigate.

I strode across the road and bent my head to get a better look behind the trees. A whimper caught my ears and I furrowed my eyebrows. When I found the golden patch I gasped and my heart melted. Behind the trees was the most adorable little golden retriever puppy with light gold fur and darker gold ears.

"Hey little guy... or girl, come on, I won't hurt you" I encouraged with that voice people use with babies. The puppy whined and crawled forward towards my outstretched hand. It sniffed my fingers before licking them with its warm rough tongue.

I bent down to pick it up and noticed it was a girl puppy. Looking around I couldn't find any passing cars and the next house wasn't for a long while but she didn't have a collar or tags anyway.

"Come on girl, you can come with me" Now I wasn't for stealing or anything but in this area she was most likely a stray.

I gently laid her in the passenger seat and closed the roof so no accidents happened and began driving again.

I stopped at a pet store to buy the essentials for the puppy and began to wonder what I should call her and decided I'd wait and ask Helena for her opinions.

I think I could quite possibly be deaf.

"SHE'S TOO FLIPPIN' ADORABLE VAL!" Helena had been at screaming level since her big brown eyes landed on the puppy. I obviously was all forgotten and therefore got no welcome back because Helena ran straight for the dog and began cradling her like a baby.

"WHAT'S HER NAME? IT NEEDS TO BE SOMETHING ADORABLE! JUST LIKE HER-!"

"Geez Helena! Calm the hell down!" I screamed at Helena. She stopped and scrunched her nose to say 'woopsies' before she sat on the ground with the puppy. "She doesn't have a name yet and I wanted wait til I got here so you could help me with one"

Helena and I sat on the floor stroking the golden puppy for the next hour shooting names at the other only be declined. We'd gone through name after name and just couldn't agree on a good one.

"Butterscotch" I turned around and realised that Max and Derrek had been privy to who knows how much of our conversation.

"What makes you think I'd name my puppy after anything you say Sparky?" Derrek smirked as he leaned against the door frame while Max immediately came over to us. He gave me a peck on the cheek, which was something new for him to do, before playing with Helena and the puppy.

"Just helping, Tadpole" he replied holding his two hands up in surrender. He then proceeded to walk straight in without a care and plopped himself down between me and Max propping one knee up and leaning his arm over it.

"Get out of my room!"

I went unnoticed.

"Come here Butterscotch" Derrek called out. The puppy sniffed the air and walked over to Derrek as though she'd known him her whole life and snuggled against his jean clad leg before her cute eyes closed shut. Hmm, well that was unexpected. Derrek, animal whisperer.

I sighed. "Fine! Butterscotch it is" I grumbled.

"So you want to go grab something to eat?" Max asked me. We were both sitting on the sofa watching Helena try to persuade Butterscotch to walk to her from Max with no success. Butterscotch had taken an unusual liking to Derrek and I'm not sure I was happy with that.

"Yeah sure" He didn't invite the other two so I assumed he'd already asked them and they declined so we let them be and left the apartment. We decided to buy some sandwiches from the campus cafe and eat it by the lake so we walked over and plopped ourselves on a bench facing it.

"You seem a bit distracted" Max said out of nowhere. I was surprised how observant he was. Over the past few months that I'd known him he'd been the ultimate best friend. He lent an ear when I was angry or a shoulder when I was down. He made me laugh and seemed to know when something was on my mind.

I almost blurted out everything that happened during my stay at home but something made me hold my tongue. What would his reaction be? From what I knew, Stingers weren't highly thought of. They were thought of something almost like a bad omen, and what if he acted out? What if he hated me and spilt my secret to the rest of the Abled community?

I was technically part Stinger.

I looked back at him and studied his creamy brown eyes. They held so much kindness and honesty that I wanted to tell him about my parents. I honestly did. I had to decide whether or not I would tell Max and even Helena.

"It's nothing" I finally replied.

I saw him deflate a little.

"You can talk to me you know... I thought you knew that?" he told me grasping both my hands in his cool ones. His thumbs skimmed across the tops of my hand where it could reach and he stared straight into my eyes not even blinking. "Is it... someone else Val?

Okay, I lost him. Was it someone else... that I wanted to talk to? No, not particularly. He seemed so focused on me I began to feel a little uncomfortable.

"I don't know what you mean Max" I responded back cocking my head to the side.

"I've seen a difference in him in the last couple of weeks and I know it's him" Max's fingers were beginning to squeeze my hands tighter, almost as though I'd run away if he didn't. I tried to pull my hands from his grasp but he wouldn't let me.

"Max you're hurting me..." I murmured. Not really, but it was becoming uncomfortable. What was up with him?

"Just tell me Val please. Is it him?" he whispered forcibly to me leaning close.

"Who the hell are you talking about Max?!" I replied speaking louder.

"Derrek! I'm talking about Derrek!" he cried back at me pulling me closer to him still.

What the hell? Was he seriously, honest to God serious?

My face contorted to surprise before I, as soft as a chainsaw, yelled "What?!" I began laughing. Not the chuckle of a proper lady, or the giggle of a school girl. Not even the laugh of a sane person but the loud, hysterical, breathless guffaw of a complete psychotic patient! I didn't even notice him let me go as I doubled over in laughter and clutched my stomach when I began to develop stitches.

I wiped the tears streaming down my eyes and took a huge breath in to steady myself. "I don't know what you're on about Max, but there is absolutely nothing and I mean nothing between me and Derrek"

He just stared at me. A slight smile crept on the corner of his lips before he lunged forward and trapped my lips against his.

Whoa! Whoa! Whoa!

His lips were smooth and lukewarm as they tried to caress mine into response and I felt his arms trace their way to clasp against my upper arms. I shoved him back and the expression I wore was probably similar to a deer caught in the headlights while his was filled with contentment.

"Max what the hell was that?!" I gasped holding my hands to my lips. His eyes shifted from side to side in shock before he out himself together.

"You uh, said there wasn't anything between you and Derrek..."

"Yeah! But a pat on the back would have been sufficient you know?" He gave a nervous chuckle before running his fingers through his blonde hair and coughed. Our time together became a little awkward so I suggested we head back and he readily agreed. Well, this was interesting...

"I'll see you around Val" Max called out to me before he quickly entered his apartment and slammed the door. I rushed back to my own apartment to find Helena and ask her what the heck was going on. I found her playing with Butterscotch, thankfully without Derrek in sight, and I began to explain everything that happened down at the lake.

"Well he obviously has a thing for you Val" she told me as soon as I finished.

"But you and Max are my best friends. I'm pretty sure I haven't given him any signs or something that I have a crush on him" I sighed in frustration and flopped on my back laying my head on her lap.

Helena chuckled. "Maybe he likes you because you're you, ever think of that? He's a nice guy Val, maybe you should just give him a chance" We sat in silence with the TV playing softly in the background of our apartment. Max was a nice guy but I wasn't sure if I wanted something to happen between us.

Night time fell upon us and the moon glowed brightly in the inky black sky. While Helena slept, I sat on the balcony watching the stars. The slight twinkle of a shining star and the bright luminosity of the moon eased my mind... just a little. Yes, I was still thinking about what to do. I couldn't believe I was still obsessing over a stolen kiss.

A walk. That's what I would do!

Popping on a leash on Butterscotch's collar I led us outside and began walking along the gravel pathway then I took the leash off Butterscotch to let her run around. Max was a great guy and was always there for me. I didn't know why I had my reservations about telling him of my nightmare but I decided I could tell him.

A screech of a hidden bat frightened Butterscotch and she yelped before running away from the sound. "Butterscotch! Stop! Come back!" I screamed as I ran after her. She was fast for a little puppy and before I knew it, I lost her in the forest.

"Damn" I whispered to myself. "Butterscotch! Butterscotch! Where are you?" I yelled. I heard my voice echo through trees and I couldn't help but shiver when the echoes from my voice in my nightmare cave haunted my mind.

"It's just a dream, Val, deep breaths" I told myself. I wondered through the trees looking for any sign of Butterscotch. The trees were thickening and I wondered if maybe I passed her or she ran in a different direction. Damnit! Being Fire-abled would have been so helpful right now.

Suddenly I stumbled into a little opened plain and I realised it was the same place where Derrek and I had our little fight. What surprised me however was that the devil himself was sitting on the far side of it leaning against a tree and stroking Butterscotch calmly.

Once again he surprises me.

He was talking to Butterscotch but I couldn't hear him or what he was saying but I was jealous that he could be so nice to my puppy and not to me. He had issues but I decided to play nice. I really wasn't up to playing water against fire tonight.

"Fancy seeing you here" I said loud enough for him to hear me.

He looked up where my voice came from and smirked, "Couldn't resist me I see"

"Right, right because you're oh so irresistible, I forgot" I replied rolling my eyes. He tapped the ground next to him and moved over to make room on the tree trunk next to him.

"Pull up some dirt and tell me why you're walking around at one in the morning" he said quietly. To say I was shocked would have been a bit of an understatement. Sweet Derrek seemed to have made another unexpected appearance so I hesitantly sat next to him.

"You tell me why you're out here first" I countered him. He was so warm. I could feel his body heat seeping through our layers of clothes and warming my skin. It was calming and I could understand why Butterscotch was drawn to him. I felt him shrug.

"I couldn't sleep"

"Same"

"Want to tell me why?" he asked me still stroking the sleeping dog.

Once again I was faced with the decision to either tell someone or not about my parents. Derrek and I weren't friends. He was close enough and isolated enough for me to know he wouldn't tell anyone else and unlike with Max, I didn't have any reservations. Though I couldn't understand why...

"I went home yesterday and received some... bothersome news. But other than that I keep having nightmares. It's the same one every night and it freaks me out so I try to put sleeping off as long as I can"

"Want to tell me about the nightmare?"Derrek asked. I looked over to him and into his golden orbs and didn't even seem to think twice. I explained to Derrek every shiver in-ducing detail about my nightmare and he only frowned more and more as I went on.

"Sounds silly right?" I asked, a little embarrassed and feel-ing a little vulnerable. He didn't say anything. He just stared straight into the dark trees stroking Butterscotch's soft fur as though in deep thought. The silence stretched on forever and I cleared my throat thinking he forgot I was here some-how.

"It's not silly Tadpole. How do you feel when you wake up?" I was surprised but told him. More silence followed.

"Sparky just tell me what's up. You're thinking so hard you might burst a vein"

"I've been having the same dreams" he told me quickly. I let it sink in before reacting because I swear he just told me that he was having the same dreams.

"What did you say?" "I'm having the same dreams, but I've been having them since I got my acceptance letter here. Lately though they've changed" he turned to look at me and his golden eyes swirled as though he was trying to read my mind or something crazy like that. "You've been in my dreams"

"How so?"

"It's exactly the same as yours except it's like I'm watching from above. I can't move or do anything but watch that man grab at your throat before I wake up" That was creep... which is saying something because I thought the nightmare itself was the definition of creepy.

We didn't speak after that. My mind just spun in circles wondering how he had the same dream as me before I potentially starred in his dream. A gust of wind blew through the trees and I shivered as the side not touching Derrek began to feel cold. It must've been hours that we'd been sitting here talking and just sitting in each other's presence.

"Cold?" Derrek's deep voice asked me. He sounded so different from the sneering smirking guy I'd come to recognise.

"A little, I'm ok though" I expected him to continue not saying anything, I didn't expect him to swing his arm around me and pull me around Butterscotch to sit between his raised knees with my back facing him. Well... this is a bit too cozy for me.

"Uh thanks Sparky, but I'm actually fine" I said trying to stand up. He wouldn't let me and gently pulled me back.

"I'm not going to jump you Tadpole. I'm just keeping you warm" he whispered into my ear blowing little tendrils of my hair as he spoke and making them tickle my ear. It was way too cozy and I'd already had one guy get a little too close for comfort so I manoeuvred my way out from his warm arms and took my place next to him again. I heard him sigh.

"Fine, fine, fine" was all he mumbled and he shot a little bundle of sticks in front of us to create a fire to keep me warm instead. I stared at him and gave him a face.

"You know, you could've done that before"

He smirked and chuckled deeply, "Yeah, I know"

Chapter 9

No nightmares.

I was shocked at my realisation that for the first time in months I hadn't had that awful nightmare that plagued my dreams. A smile flickered in the corners of my mouth and I rubbed a hand roughly over my tired eyes.

Maybe that was the trick of not having nightmares? Staying up late enough to be overly exhausted that I didn't even have the brain power to dream. Whatever it was I was overjoyed to wake up in high spirits. I skipped over to the shower and afterwards dressed in a bright yellow plain t-shirt and denim short shorts while slipping on yellow converses. I was in a happy mood and wanted to portray that with my clothes too! I quickly ate breakfast and dashed off with a bright eyed Helena to history.

Bang!

And there is Mr Arbit, as always.

"Sorry I'm late class! Please quieten down we have a fair bit to discuss today and I'm sure you'd rather pretend to listen to me instead of reading the chapter in your text books!" Mr Arbit yelled all in one breath.

Today's class was concentrated on The Control. Mr Arbit spoke about the high members of The Control which consisted of one Abled of each ability to make the main decisions and deliver punishments.

Before The Stinger Eradication there were five high members, but obviously there were only four now. The Stinger high member was a man called Malum, he was kicked out of The Control for his despicable plots and train of thoughts. Malum had thought that Stingers would've been the better option for the high members seeing as their ability would have been the better powers to deliver punishments. He had plotted several times to over throw the high members but was always caught before he could go ahead.

"Mr Arbit sir, if this Malum guy was caught so many times plotting against The Control why did it take so long for him to be kicked out?" A student called out, I wasn't surprised to see it was Colin.

"Good question Colin" Mr Arbit called back. Seeing as Colin always had questions Mr Arbit knew him on a first name basis. "Every group of Abled voted on the person who will be high member and Malum was always voted back"

This made sense. Considering it was a modern day government, despite the fact it was a government for people with super natural abilities. After Malum was over thrown from The Control there were no Stinger high member and soon after that was the beginning of The Stinger Eradication.

"Hey Val" I turned and saw Max standing further away from me with a grimace held on his face.

"Hey Max, what's up?" I replied falling in step with him. We had water skills next and were headed over to the pool room.

"Um, I just wanted to, you know, apologise about what happened down at the lake yesterday. I shouldn't have kissed you like that" he apologised scratching his head.

I gave him a lopsided smile and punched his shoulder. "No need to worry Max. Honestly, it's fine"

He smiled back and heaved a sigh in relief. "Thanks Val. It's just that... I like you. I know it's pretty obvious now and I'm putting myself out on a limb but I was just wondering if you would, well, go out to dinner with me one time?"

"Like a date?"

"Yeah, like a date" I looked at Max and he was really nervous. If the light sheen of sweat across his forehead didn't tell me otherwise his fidgeting hands were. So, I thought about it. Helena said that I should give him a chance last night, and she was right. Max had been an awesome friend and I even told myself that I would tell him about the nightmare. I wasn't ready to tell anyone about my parents yet.

"Sure. Why not," I told him. He was all smiles to the class and even opened the door for me like a gentleman.

Water skills was difficult today.

Today we were manipulating water to become weapons and compacting them hard enough to pierce skin, almost like ice but without freezing it. I was way too tired from staying up with Derrek and had a little trouble keeping the molecules compacted.

All around me students held swords, maces, shields, whips and bow and arrows all made of pure water. It was quite a sight to see, if it was done right. I was holding a bow of compacted water molecules trying to shoot the target with the water arrow but I couldn't concentrate and the arrow would burst into a shower of droplets.

"Valerie, you seem a little off today" Ms Flumine noted, "You will need this skill for Combat class so I suggest you take it easy now to avoid major accidents in class" Combat class! Damn I forgot about that. I was so exhausted I didn't know how I will handle it. Water skills ended and we shuffled forward to the auditorium. As we entered I was still awestruck at the interior.

The desert, forest, lake and infirmary were still here and today the class settled in the middle.

" Alright class let's get moving! So earlier you all learned about 'element solidify'. Today you will be partnered up and this is the technique, the only technique, that you will be using to attack your partner. Once again I am asking for nothing life threatening" Coach Shulk boomed.

For every combat class I'd been partnered with Colin so I was surprised when Coach Shulk called my name and partnered me with Derrek. I looked around for him and saw him at the back of the class not even moving. He looked dangerous with his tight black shirt and leather jacket that hung just above his low slung jeans, it seemed to match his brooding look. I walked over to him and smiled. He glanced down at me and looked back at the coach. Ah, so jackass Derrek is back again I see. Damn.

Derrek was like an enigma. Once I thought I had him all figured out, his whole personality changed and I didn't know what to think of it. Since day one here, my thoughts of Derrek had flip flopped back and forth so many times I might need to clone myself just to keep up with it. The coach finished partnering up the class and everyone walked off to different locations. Without glancing at me to see if I was following Derrek immediately turns to walk towards the desert scene. Just great.

I follow after him and I could feel the hydration around me disappearing. The desert scene seemed to have been modified to actually dry out almost every bit of moisture and I wasn't liking how this would turn out. Luckily we were the closest to the forest and I knew I would be able to collect moisture from there.

"What's wrong Tadpole? Feeling like a fish out of water?" I turned to face Derrek, he was smirking at me. I scoffed, what else was new. As I watched him I noticed he positioned himself between two mounds of flame spurting dirt. Almost like mini volcanoes.

"Maybe" I told him truthfully, "But I can still kick your ass Sparky" Just then the twin volcanoes spat out two large orange flames and Derrek quickly swiped them. He swirled his hands in a circle as though he was rolling a ball between his hands and the flames mixed together to shape into a large flaming sword.

The sword handle looked almost as though it was molten rock with cracks throughout showing the glowing fire within and the blade, although it looked solid, had flames licking all around the edges. Derrek held it with two hands and spun it around his head before waiting to see what I would pull out from a desert.

I concentrated hard. I wasn't in my element, like he was, where my element would be readily available. I swung my hand across my body and faced it behind me with my fingers spread apart towards the forest, always keeping my eyes on Derrek in case he decided to play dirty. I collected the water within the plants practically dehydrating them and strung it together to create a long sturdy whip. I couldn't gather enough water to create something more so this would have to do.

I focused my ability and the handle of the whip hardened to the point of being frozen. All the way down the hardened water whip little droplets of water dripped down to the end and splattered against the ground. Derrek laughed and stood in an offensive stance, "You better hope that little whip of yours can with stand against fire" then he lunged towards me.

I swung my whip backwards and lashed it toward him to try to fend him off but there was no use. He was very quick, something I hadn't realised when we first fought. He sliced across my left arm and deepened into my shoulder just when I tried to jump backwards. The burning blade carved through my flesh while the flames ate at the surrounding skin and burnt through my yellow t-shirt.

I screamed and held around the unharmed skin. What the hell!

I didn't have time to moan about it because he was back into position and was about to attack again. With my right arm I swung the whip back and aimed it at his sword. The thong, or main part of the whip, twirled around the blade of the flaming sword like a vine. Steamed sizzled at the contact and I grimaced hoping the water would kill the flame, but I was so wrong. The steam thickened as I tried to concentrate the water around the sword. He seemed to be thinking the same as me because before I knew it the flames of the sword burst outwards, growing in size. It grew and sizzled until the thong grew slack and fell to the ground

His flaming sword had evaporated my whip!

"Sh*t!" I cried.

He gave a deep smirk and went to swipe at me again now that I was weaponless. I tried grasping at all the dry moisture in the air and managed to piece together a pathetic excuse of a shield. It was small and circular, barely able to cover my face and shoulders, but it should deflect the majority of his hit.

Derrek threw his sword in an arch and the power behind it knocked me to my back. Pain shot through my injured shoulder and I could feel the blood mixing among the third degree burns. The flaming sword pierced through my water shield cutting the side of my face. The sword was stuck so I used that moment to spin the shield around and tear the sword from Derrek's grasp.

"What are you going to do Tadpole? You can't touch fire" Derrek's deep voice mocked. He was right. I couldn't do anything with his element so I rearranged the water particles making the sword drop and my whip was back again, if not a little shorter.

"Do your worst Tadpole" Derrek chuckled. I twirled the whip above my head, feeling the muscles in my arm ache and whipped it at lightning speed towards Derrek's handsome face. At first I thought he was just going to stand there and take it but just as the popper of the whip was about to slice his face he'd constructed a blazing shield to deflect my strike.

I cried in frustration. It was like Derrek was toying with me and I was growing tired of his antics. I turned to gather as much water from the forest but a searing, burning pain was eating at my throat.

"Never turn your back on your opponent" Derrek whispered in my ear. He was holding his, once again, fiery sword close to my throat. He wasn't slicing me, nor holding it directly on my skin, but the sheer closeness was blistering the delicate skin of my neck.

"You had better move that" I whispered back being careful not to make any sudden movement in case my own stupidity cost me my voice box.

"Or what...?"

I had nothing. What could do I do? The air was completely void of moisture and Derrek literally had me by the throat. "Okay, okay I give in. You win" I conceded. The flames disappeared from my throat and I felt at the blistering skin. "Ouch" I murmured quietly.

"Sorry, but I wasn't going to take it easy on you just because you're a girl. You'd better go to the infirmary and have the Healers look at you" Derrek said looking at the damage he did.

"Hey, you okay?" Max asked as he leaned against the chair I was sitting in. I was sitting in the infirmary while Kayla, one of the Healers, worked on me. In no time at all the blisters and burns from my throat, arm and shoulder were gone and the gash was a faded pink line that would go away in a few days.

"I'm good. Derrek just had the advantage was all" I answered. Max wore fitted jeans with a white t-shirt and blue and black checked flannel that he wore unbuttoned over the top. He held out a hand and I took it as he helped me out of the chair.

"So, about that date, how does tonight suit you?" he asked as we walked back to our apartments.

"I don't know. I'm so sore from Combat I don't know if I can handle more than sitting on the sofa" I joked with him.

"That's okay. How about I bring take away and we have a lazy night in. That is, if you're up for it" he suggested. It was so sweet of him and I agreed a bit warily.

Tonight could either make or break our friendship.

Chapter 10

The spray of hot water that showered me eased my taut muscles. I was aching all over and my shoulder was still a little stiff but the hot shower relieved the pain a little. I'd probably been in the shower for an hour, just letting the water run over my skin and letting my thoughts run wild before trickling down the drain with the rest of the water.

I opened the door and watched as the steam that collected in the shower burst out and coiled around the ceiling before disappearing. I felt refreshed. Water, in any form, always made me feel better and having the cool moist air and hot steam swirling around me made me feel stronger.

Grabbing a fluffy towel I dried my damp skin and wrapped it around me before heading into the cooler bedroom to find something date worthy for tonight. I didn't want to wear something that would give Max the wrong idea, but I did want to try to look decent enough to say 'yes this is a date, not just a dinner between best friends'.

Helena had told me she'd study in the library to 'give us some alone time' so I couldn't ask her for her opinion. Eventually I decided on a pair of white jeans and a loose silk top that dipped a little lower at the back. It had a swirling pattern with dark and light blues and since it was Max's favourite colour I decided 'why not?' I didn't bother with shoes but I did fix my hair so that it hung down my back and framed my eyes with eyeliner. Lastly I draped the necklace Max gave me on my birthday around my neck. I stepped back and looked at myself in the mirror. That should do.

I glanced over at the clock and saw it was nearly seven. I was starving and the grumbling of my stomach made it embarrassingly obvious. A knock on the door caught my attention and I jumped up to answer it. I swung it open and found a smiling Max holding two bags of Chinese food.

"Come on in Max" I greeted him brightly. The food smelt delicious and even though it sounded awful for me to even think about it, I was a little more excited to see the food than Max.

"Hey, wow Val you look beautiful" Max said looking me up and down. I stood to the side and let him through.

"Just put them on the coffee table. We can eat on the sofa" I instructed him, half ignoring his compliment. He did as I said and I sat next to him after closing the door with a soft click.

"I didn't know what you'd want so I pretty much bought everything" he told me with a little chuckle. I laughed and peeked into the bags. They were both filled with containers crammed with different food plus a huge bag of prawn crackers.

"Wow, I think you read my mind Max. I'm starving so maybe this will just fill us both up!" I joked. But I swear to God I was telling the truth.

"Well, bon appétit Val" he saluted clinking his bottle of cola against my bottle of lemonade. I clinked back then dug straight into the first container I could find.

"Oh my goodness... I feel like an overinflated balloon" I moaned as I sat back against the cushions. Max laughed at me and poked my stomach softly.

"Where the hell do you stash all of the food you eat? You don't look as if you just ate three quarters of the food"

I laughed loudly and poked him back, "Shush you, I was so hungry!"

I absentmindedly rubbed my healing shoulder but Max saw the movement. "Your shoulder still bothering you Val?" he asked me a little concerned. "Maybe Kayla didn't do a proper job"

"No, no, no I'm fine. It's just a little stiff. But enough about me how'd you do in Combat? What weapon did you decide on?"

"Double headed axe" he replied taking out two fortune cookies and handing me one, "I did okay. One side kept on melting or something. I was against Colin too! I swear Ms Shulk has something out for me because I always end up having to fight against him and he's deceptively good"

I imagined how that fight could've gone and smiled. Colin was almost an expert when it came to using his abilities with rocks. At least when I fought Derrek it wasn't like his fire was as solid as rock. Although it was pretty damn close!

With my urging, Max continued to tell me all about his fight and by the end I was in hysterics! I was laughing so hard I had tears streaming down my face. Max was laughing too but covered his face to hide the shame of trying to slice Colin but losing concentration and having his axe splash Colin like a bucket of water. Only after apologising was he knocked sideways by Colin's mace.

"I swear to God if I'm ever paired with him again or fighting him, there will be zero mercy" Max shouted melodramatically shaking a fist to the ceiling. His dramatics caused me to burst into another set of hysterics and by the time I finished I was panting for fresh air.

"I love the way you laugh" Max said out of the blue, "It's like you don't hold back from what's funny and it's so contagious" I smiled. I'd never been told something like that but by the way he was smiling at me it was hard to deny what he was saying. We were both leaning our heads against the cushions looking at one another with our arms almost touching, a giggle or deep chuckle escaping out throats every once in a while.

"You really are something different you know?" Max said softly. "I can't explain it. Ever since that first day I saw you it was like I needed to get to know you"

"You thought that while I was on the ground shouting at Derrek for bumping into me?" I joked.

Max laughed and rolled his eyes, "Yes, yes that's totally what I was thinking" he replied sarcastically. Silence followed. It wasn't awkward and neither of us minded it. We just sat there watching the others movements before Max leaned forward.

His face came close to mine and his eyes flew down to my lips before resting back to my eyes again almost like he was silently asking for permission. I licked my lips and kept my eyes on his giving him the acknowledgement he needed. Slowly he lifted his hand to touch my cheek, rubbing a thumb over the curve of my jaw before bending to bring his lips to mine.

He stopped a breath away waiting for me to accept his kiss. So I bent my head and connected our lips. Tingles spread through my lips and down my spine making me feel as though the air was suddenly humid. The kiss was short and sweet and when I pulled away he simply leaned his forehead against mine with his eyes still closed, as though revelling in the memory.

"Thank you" he murmured opening his eyes.

"For the kiss?" I asked.

"No, for giving me another chance, but the kiss was pretty amazing"

I smiled and pecked him on the lips once more. "No problem" I whispered. After our little make out session we watched a movie on the TV with Butterscotch lazily swinging her tail side to side on the floor by our feet. The sound of the door opening and closing made us jump and we found a haggard looking Helena dragging herself through the apartment.

"Night guys" she mumbled before walking through to our bedroom.

"It's getting pretty late" I mention noticing that was midnight already. How time flies.

"Yeah, I guess" Max agreed disappointedly, "We should do this again another time" I agreed with a smile and walked him to the door. He dropped his head and pressed his lips to mine as a goodnight kiss and turned to walk down the corridor with a happy grin on his face.

I closed the door and stared blankly into the open space as I touched my fingertips to my lips. I cleaned up and switched off the lights before heading to the bedroom. Helena was lying face down spread out like a starfish diagonally across her bed as though she just fell straight down and passed out. Poor girl.

I dressed in sweats and a tank top and hopped into bed. I closed my eyes ready for sleep over take over when a flash of the hooded face from my nightmare popped against my eyelids. Damn, I forgot all about the nightmare.

Surely one nightmare free night was all I was going get? I would consider that after months of repetitive nightmares, having one dream free night was all I was going to have. No, I just needed to get it into my head that it was just a dream and all I needed to do was take control.

"Come here Butterscotch" I whispered patting the space next to me. Butterscotch trotted over and jumped up onto the bed and immediately curled up next to my chest. I cuddled her and laid my head back down on the soft pillow then, without permission, my eyelids slid closed.

I was standing in my nightmare cave and I felt like bursting into tears. Why? Why am I always here and why can't anything change? I walked forward already knowing what will happen and who I'll bump into, but for some reason, when I walk into the larger chamber of the cave I find myself not looking towards the shadowy area that holds the mysterious, evil hooded man. I look up towards the roof of the cave only to be greeted by protruding rocks and bats hanging upside down.

I hadn't noticed before but the roof held plenty of bats that peeked down at me from the gap of their cocooning wings. Their beady eyes sent chills down my spine and I quickly looked away to be greeted by the hooded man.

"I will find you Valerie" he hissed before and, as always, lounged for my throat again.

As always I woke up with a throbbing pain between my temples. The creepy feeling of someone tapping into my brain made me shiver and goosebumps crawled across my exposed skin. I don't think I'll ever get used to this horrible feeling.

I laid in bed staring at the white ceiling between the vines that had began to crawl across it and rubbed at my fatigued eyes. Today was the anniversary that Malum was kicked out of The Control and therefore was considered a public holiday for the Abled community. There were no classes and instead the university held a fete out on the grounds.

Today was the perfect day to be outdoors. The sky was dyed an azure blue with pearly white clouds streaked across it, as though a painter decided that simple puffs of cloud were boring. The sun shone brightly on the brilliant green grass and a light breeze rustled the leaves that hung from the trees. It was still early and all over the campus grounds the festivities for the fete were being set up like a mini carnival. I was excited for it to begin. I hadn't really been to a carnival before and the closest experience I had were all from TV.

I showered and threw on a pair of dark jeans and matched it with a loose black t-shirt I'd cut up to fall off my shoulder. Helena began stirring and I ran over and up onto her bed only to start jumping around her to wake the girl up. "Grhmm" she mumbled.

"Wake up sunshine! You're not one to sleep in" I called out.

"I know! But I studied hard last night! I'd ask why you're in such a happy mood but I could guess it was because of a certain Max you were making out with last night" Helena retorted with a grin. Suddenly she swiped at my feet making me collapse on top of her earning a groan from the both of us.

"Okay... not my best idea" she groaned from under my legs.

We began laughing and I shoved her off the bed telling her to shower and get dressed while I cooked us waffles. She rolled her eyes but smiled as she skipped off to the bathroom. I ran my fingers through my hair not even bothering to brush it then wandered off to the kitchen.

"Knock knock!" Max called out as he and Derrek strode into my apartment as though they owned the place. Max wore a huge grin and had an extra bounce in his step as he walked over to me and kissed my cheek. "Something smells good!" He said sniffing the air and giving me puppy dog eyes.

"Oh fine, sit down and I'll make some for the both of you" I rolled my eyes.

I eyed Derrek. He was quieter than usual and seemed preoccupied. He didn't smirk or make some comment, he just avoided my eyes and sat at the far end of the table.

"Good morning boys" Helena called out as she bounced through the bedroom door seeming like her regular hyperactive self. The guys waved and she plonked herself on a chair singing about waffles. I finished cooking and placed the huge plate of cooked waffles in the centre of the table where it was bombarded by Max and Helena.

"You eating Sparky?"

He didn't answer me, instead just grabbing a waffle and eating it plain. I shrugged my shoulders. Max had left a space for me to sit by him so I sat in the spare seat and he grinned at me. I couldn't help but smile at how easy it was to make him happy.

"So when were you two heading to the fete?" Max asked after gulping down a mouthful of crushed waffle.

I shrugged, "Whenever they open I suppose. I'd never been to a fete before" In the corner of my eye I saw Butterscotch happily wag her tail in front of Derrek as he ripped up pieces of waffle and threw it down for her to catch. I rolled my eyes. She was going to get so spoilt soon, she had her own bowl of food but was completely ignoring it for food and attention from Derrek.

We continued talking about the different rides and what else would be there. Helena washed up and we lounged around the apartment until the voices of the crowd outside grew louder.

"What do you say? Want to head out now?" Everyone nodded, except Derrek who seemed determined to stare at me. This was a little more disturbing than when he was ignoring me to be honest. I kneeled down to scratch Butterscotch's coat, "Be a good girl ok?"

"Come on beautiful" Max urged me swinging his arm around my shoulders and leading us outside. We walked down the stairs seeing as the elevator was jam packed with students waiting to go outside and just when we were about to step outside Derrek took hold of my arm.

"Can I talk to you for a minute Tadpole?" he asked me quietly. I looked at Max who was eyeing Derrek questioningly.

"Sure" I answered and slipped out from under Max's warm arm. "I'll meet you and Helena at the fete okay?" Max nodded and walked with Helena out of our sight.

"So what's up?" I asked Derrek folding my arms across my body.

He nodded his head towards the forest and I rolled my eyes. We seemed to have this issue where we only have moments in the damn forest, but I followed him nonetheless. Only until the chatter and laughter of the noisy crowd was dulled by the thick trees did he stop and turn to look at me.

"Did you have nightmares again last night?" he asked me straight out.

"Yes"

"Were they the same? Exactly the same?" he was staring straight into my eyes like he normally did when he was focused on something and once again I felt as though he was trying to read my mind.

"Yes"

He sighed loudly. "So everything happened exactly the same? You didn't do anything different?" I thought about it and remembered how I looked at the hanging bats. Surely that didn't really mean anything right? I mentally shrugged, "The only thing different that happened was that I looked up at the ceiling and saw bats before the man said he'd find me"

Derrek stayed quiet. I thought that maybe he'd go into one of his silent moments again so I busied myself gazing around at the forest. I watched how the rays of sunlight peeked through the canopy above and shot streams of light throughout the area.

"You looked at me"

I spun around to look at Derrek. "Huh? No, I was just looking at the trees"

"No, in your dream. You looked at me" I stared at him wondering what he was talking about. When I couldn't figure it out I asked him. He sighed with frustration and roughly scratched the back of his neck.

"I told you I've been like a viewer to your nightmares. I didn't think I was literally in your dreams but when last night's dream changed a little I needed to know if you had changed it and it wasn't me dreaming it up"

"Okay... so what?" I asked him confused, "So what if you're somehow magically stalking me in my dreams. It doesn't mean anything and there's nothing we can do"

"Maybe" I was getting a headache from his damn riddles and walked over to him,

"Come on Sparky there's no point in over thinking it. Let's go have some fun!" I grabbed his wrist and began pulling him towards the fete and out of the gloomy forest. The sound of carnival music, shouts and people laughing filled my ears as we stepped out of the forest and I my lips curved into a huge smile at the sight before me. A large ferris wheel stood tall and in the centre of the fete while a spinning vortex spun people around so fast they were nothing but a blur.

There were contests, games and stalls that sold food and others that had games that offered prizes. I felt like a little girl that wanted to go crazy in Disneyworld! "Come on Sparky, let's go!" I cried tightening my grip on his wrist and running towards the first stall I could see. The stall was decorated with cheap plush toys varying in size, much like the others. It was the game where you squirt a water gun into the mouth of a clown until the balloon above its head burst.

I eyed Derrek and grinned which he returned with a smirk, "Oh you're going down Tadpole"

We both grabbed a gun and began squirting the clown. I didn't realise how good he was and I wasn't going to cheat but... oh why not? I flicked my index finger and his stream of water began veering to the right in an 'L' shape.

"Hey!" he shouted in surprise.

"I want that panda okay?!" I laughed. I could hear him laughing and the next thing I know my stream of water began steaming then evaporated just as it met the mouth of the clown. "No! Sparky! I want that panda!"

Neither one of us were giving in so I turned the gun on him and began squirting the life out of him. "What the...!" I guess

I should've realised that he'd do that same and soon enough the both of us were soaking wet.

"So...who... won?" I huffed to the amused man behind the counter of the stall. He checked, even though neither of the balloons burst and announced that Derrek won. I pouted and rolled my eyes, that's karma for cheating I guess.

The man gave Derrek the panda I wanted but then Derrek turned to me. "Here you go Tadpole, even though you cheated" he eyed me, "I wouldn't be caught dead with a stuffed toy"

I smiled and grabbed the panda hugging it tightly, "I will call you Patches" I announced, looking into the panda's golden eyes that reminded me of Derrek's eyes. I smiled at Derrek and just as he began returning the smile I saw him stop himself and stuck his grim expression on again. It was as though he didn't want us to have a happy moment between us. Looks like he had another mood swing again, I sighed.

"Hey Val!" I turned at the sound of my name and saw Max coming towards us. He swung his arm around my neck possessively "Want to go on the spinning vortex thing?" he asked pointing at the huge spinning metal contraption. I nodded eagerly and turn to ask Derrek if he wanted to join us but he was already gone.

"Woooo!!!" Max shouted as we stood against the cushioned walls and it spun us around at an alarming speed. I felt the skin of my face push against my skull as I stuck to the wall by the force of gravity. I began laughing and tried looking out at the crowd as we tipped from side to side.

A flash of bright red caught my attention and I thought it was a fire but when we spun around again it was gone. There must've been a game including fire, I thought. After the ride Max and I were walking between the stalls wondering what to do next. There were so many colourful and interesting stalls it was like a wonderland. My stomach growled and Max laughed.

"Well, I guess we know what to do next" we walked into the main area that was surrounded by masses of different food selections. The aroma of sweet, salty, cooked and uncooked foods wafted through the air and my stomach grumbled again at the variety of choices. What could I say, I loved my food!

We grabbed a hot dog each and sat at a dirty empty picnic bench. As I took a bite I thought about Derrek. He was so mysterious and always seemed to want an invisible wall between us. I'd seen a glimpse of his caring and funny side but it seemed that as soon as he realised it was showing he'd close it up as tight as a clam.

Max was so open and funny with me, he cared and made it obvious, very obvious, of his feelings. I liked him but I couldn't help but feel more connected with Derrek. Even if he was a mysterious a$s sometimes the underlying care he had when he asked about my dreams stuck with me.

I could hear Max talking to me but couldn't listen to him. I was distracted by the flash of bright red that I'd seen on the spinning vortex. I moved my head around to try and see what game it was but stopped when I saw it was actually a girl. A girl who seemed a little too close for my liking to Derrek.

She was tall from what I could see, much taller than me. Her hair was a fiery red with bursts of orange that rolled in neat waves down her back and it almost looked as though her head was on fire. Her skin looked as though it used to be porcelain but had a slight tan to it as though her hair itself had been her own personal sunshine.

Her body was one every woman would be jealous of, not actually being too skinny but with curves in all the right places. I was surprised at the surge of jealousy at this unknown woman, I mean I didn't know her!

"Val? You okay Val?" Max's voice broke through my own crazy thoughts and I turned to see his concerned eyes staring at me.

"Sorry, what?"

"I asked if you were okay?"

"Oh, yeah I'm fine" I lied. "Hey, uh do you know who that is? I've never seen her before"

Max squinted at the beautiful, fiery red head as he tried to see who she was. "Oh, yeah that's Sarah. She and Derrek are both in Fire Skills together"

"Hmm" I mumbled.

"STEP UP, STEP UP TO PLAY THE DISTRACTION CONTEST!" An announcer yelled a few stalls away. Everyone turned to his screaming voice and moved along to see what it was all about. We all crowded around the balding, big bellied man who explained the rules.

There would be couples lined up with one standing behind the other. The person at the back had to hold their element above their partner's head and keep it there for as long as they can. Across from them another person were allowed to do anything, ANYTHING, they can think of to distract them into dropping the element on their partner's head.

"Want to have a go?" Max asked me.

"Can we watch the other's first so I fully understand?" He nodded and we watched, gasped and laughed as one by one someone dropped their element on their partner's head. The worst and funniest was watching Colin drop a rock on his partner's head as a girl flashed her chest at him.

However, I grew more and more jealous when I saw that every round was won by Derrek and this 'Sarah' girl. Every-time they won she'd jump up and hug Derrek tightly rubbing her voluptuous chest against his own firm one.

"Come on" I growled at Max as I dragged him next to Derrek and Sarah. "I'll hold and you sit"

"Okay, I'm trusting you Val!" I flashed him a tight grin and collected the water from a bucket next to me.

"And three, two, one, HOLD" The announcer cried.

Rocks, piles of dirt, water and spiralling balls of fire hovered in the air above trusting friends and one by one the people across them would distract them. Squeals, shouts and laughter erupted when their friend dropped their element down and soon it was between me and Derrek.

My distracter was horrible. A bulky boy who seemed like he was trying to grow a beard but simply didn't have the facial hair for it was shouting out sexist comments and grabbing the front of his jeans as he thrust it towards me. I lifted an eyebrow and sent part of my element at his face throwing him backwards.

"Does that mean we win?" Sarah screamed at the announcer.

"No darlin' it has to fall on the partner's head" Time passed and no one could distract me or Derrek and soon enough Sarah was the one trying to distract me.

"You know Max, I don't understand why you'd want to date a girl like Val. At least Derrek here has good taste"

"Sarah!" Derrek warned her. His ball of orange flames was turned red and I remembered at my birthday party how he mentioned his fire changed according to his emotions.

"Well it's true babe. Val is... is... well look at her! Someone like you would never go for someone like her. What you need Derrek is a fiery rebel like me!" she cried with an evil giggle. I was fuming and I didn't even care about the contest anymore.

"What makes you think he'd go for someone like you Sarah?" I yelled back saying her name childishly as the water above wobbled a little.

"Because Derrek and I have more than amazing time spent together and he wouldn't dare have his lips anywhere near yours!" she screamed back making it blatantly obvious what she meant by 'time spent together'.

"Sarah! Shut up!" Derrek shouted and his ball of red flames began to spurt wildly like solar eruptions on the surface of the sun.

I honestly don't know why she hated me as much as I hated her when we technically hadn't even met yet but I didn't give a damn. All I wanted at that moment was to prove to her that she wasn't God's gift to all men, it may have been a childish train of thought but I was too pumped on adrenaline and anger to care. I turned to face Derrek next to me and stuck my arm out to grab the back of his head bringing his lips down to meet mine.

I managed to see Derrek's flames turn to purple and disappear sending sparks of ember falling down on Sarah's head but barely heard the splash of water and Max shout before I shut my eyes to enjoy the kiss. His lips were softer than I thought and I licked his bottom lip asking for permission. His hot rough hands tugged on my waist and I flew against his body as he deepened the kiss.

"Get a room!"

I jumped back and my cheeks flushed a deep red as I saw the crowd smiling or chuckling. Some guys were even wolf whistling and screaming "Oh yes Derrek!" in a high pitched girly voice.

"Now that's what I call a distraction!" The announcer cried.

Chapter 11

Oh dear Lord, what have I done…?

I stared at Derrek's surprised eyes that darkened to a deeper gold. I could feel my eyes grow wider and wider until they stretched to the point of hurting. The crowds' shouts and hollers no longer reached my ears and I was surrounded by silence as I stared at Derrek. Suddenly strong arms wrapped themselves around my shoulders and hugged me tight.

"Not the distraction I'd come up with but definitely effective nonetheless" Max shouted near my ear making my eardrum ring a little. I turned to him and only realised then that he was soaking wet.

"Max! Get off me, your clothes are dripping wet!" I laughed. My emotions were flying everywhere! I had a happy Max, who has a massive crush on me, even though I kissed Derrek. I had a surprised and confused Derrek who had just given me the most amazing and heart stopping kiss I'd ever experienced despite the fact that we were interrupted! Then finally,

I had a pissed off red head who was glaring at me like her life depended on it.

"I... uh..." was pretty much all I could get out from my frozen lips which still felt burnt from Derrek's lips.

"I thought Sarah almost had you but then BAM, you spin around and used the ultimate distraction to win us the contest" Max gloated, "Well, second ultimate" he winked. I was stammering again and I felt like an idiot. I couldn't, for the life of me, string two comprehensible words together!!! At Max's statement Derrek's eyes burnt like molten lava and glowered at me.

"Congratulations to the winners!" The announcer boomed and threw fifty dollars to both Max and myself. By the time I looked back at Derrek he and Sarah were already gone, I couldn't even spot Sarah's flaming hair.

"Come on Val the day is still young! Let's look for Helena and check out the games" Max said steering me towards the clearest path out. We eventually found Helena at a little plant nursery and made our way around the fete. "Hey there's a game of volleyball over there!" Helena cried pointing to the outer parts of the fete. We ran over to watch the end of the current game the students were playing and to my disgust I found Sarah competing.

"Let's just go" I murmured suddenly losing interest in the game.

"What, why?" Max and Helena asked in unison. I shrugged my shoulders and began to turn when the most annoying voice perked up.

"Well, well, well... look who it is. Little Miss Distraction" Sarah's snooty voice called out.

"You know her?" Helena asked.

"Kind of" I grumbled, sighing deeply, being around her seemed to drain me from all my patience. The ball was served into Sarah's side and was set up high into position. Sarah ran up to spike it down towards the other team and a skinny pixie haired girl dived into the sand to try to save it but ended up with a mouthful of sand instead.

"Hell yeah!" Sarah and her team mates shouted as they hi-fived each other. "Is there no one who can beat us!?" I rolled my eyes at her boisterous personality but secretly was happy that Derrek wasn't with her. It actually surprised me that he was even hanging out with her considering he seemed like the lone wolf type of guy... except when he hangs with Max, Helena and myself.

I looked around standing on my toes to try and see if Derrek was hanging around but he was nowhere to be seen. I don't know why I cared really, but something about what Sarah was mocking me with during the contest disturbed me. She seemed pretty close to Derrek and I didn't even know he was friends with anyone else. I had always thought that Max was pretty much his only friend but I guess I was wrong. My mind turned to Max and how he hadn't even blinked an eye at me kissing Derrek. He thought I was doing it just to win and I knew that even if we were dating he'd act the same too.

This just proved how trusting Max was and I felt a little warmness touch my heart at the thought. Trust was something really important to me and always had been since I came into the care of Serena and Troy. Max trusted me without batting an eye and here I was second guessing whether or not I should tell him about some crazy nightmares. For some reason it felt like they were a secret between me and Derrek.

Oompf!

My thoughts were interrupted when the volleyball bounced off the side of my head and landed at my feet. "Oopsies, that was totally an accident" Sarah 'apologised', "Pass the ball if you can get it this far"

I snorted, her insults were pretty pathetic and I dropped down to pick up the ball. I threw it into the air and served it straight at her pretty damn hard. Her eyes widened and she ducked just in time for it to miss her mess of curls.

"Whoa! I didn't know you knew how to play volleyball Val?" Helena gasped.

I shrugged, "My volleyball team in high school was the best in the state" I heard a deep chuckle and my eyes quickly flicked to the wonder that is Derrek. He stood far away but close enough to overhear the conversation and had his arms crossed over his sculpted chest.

"Hey! That was an awesome overhand serve! Did you want to join our team?" the skinny pixie haired girl asked me. I didn't even see her walk up to me but I suddenly noticed the crowd that was watching their game was intent on my answer encouraging me to join in the game.

"Oh... uh, no that's okay" I declined as heat flushed onto my face. I had a bad habit of getting far too intent on the game when I'm playing.

"Come on Val, I'll even join you!" Helena piped in with a huge smile on her face.

"Me too!" Came Max's voice. I was caving in. I loved the game and with Helena and Max by my side I wouldn't feel so embarrassed I guess.

"Er... okay, fine. But just ONE game!"

Sarah gave an odd evil laugh as she bounced the volleyball up into the air and catching it again while we made our way to the others. The crowd had grown but I could sense Derrek's gaze on my back as I walked. We slipped off our shoes and spread out across the sand court.

"Here, you can go first since you have a mean serve" one the guys on my team offered throwing me the ball. I caught it and walked to the back corner behind the line that showed where the court ended.

I stretched out my arms waiting for everyone to get into position. A student posing as referee blew his whistle and I breathed in, I liked to make the opposing team squirm before I served so I counted eight seconds before I tossed the ball up high spinning it slightly. It hovered for a moment before it fell back down and with as much strength as I could muster I swung my arm in an arch and sent it flying over the net.

Sarah and her team mates had probably thought I had a lucky hit earlier because by the way it flew straight into the face of a tall blonde girl and knocked her backwards, they weren't expecting that. The crowd whooped and cheered and I couldn't help a little smirk slide onto the corner of my mouth. I think it was time to let some steam off.

I'd served four times without the other team being able to get the ball back over so by the fifth time I was feeling a little sorry for them and served the ball a little softer letting the other team have a chance.

We were winning by one point with the score being twenty-five to twenty-four so if we won the next point we'd win the game. Helena served the ball with a powerful strike and Sarah's team scrambled into position. The ball was hit up to be set into a good spot for Sarah, who seemed to be the captain of her team, to spike it back.

Sarah, in all her bouncing-chested glory, ran forward swinging her arms backwards and jumped up high. Her right arm swung up and slammed the ball straight down towards the pixie haired girl on my team. It bounced hard off her head and rebounded up into the air. I chased after it out of the court and jumped, hammering the ball upwards and back into our court before I landed in the sand. Max ran up and managed to tip it with his fingertips. The ball scraped over the top of the net and hit the sand just as a huge boy tried diving for it.

The crowd erupted in cheers and whistles as we won and I had to say, I was feeling pretty proud of myself. I hugged Helena but was scooped up bridal style by Max as he yelled our victory. I was laughing at his over hyper response to winning a simple volleyball game and didn't realise I was subconsciously scanning the crowd for a certain dark haired, brooding man.

I spotted Derrek at the front of the crowd with his famous smirk and clapping lightly as he stared straight into my eyes sending little butterflies flying head first at the walls of my stomach. Suddenly it felt wrong to be staring so intently at Derrek while being held by Max so I kicked my legs enough to let Max know I wanted to get down and he gently plopped me on my feet.

"You got lucky Valerie" snapped Sarah as she stalked away from the court and the crowds.

"Sheesh, what crawled up her dainty little ass and died?" I asked no one in particular.

"Forget her, she's got issues" Helena rolled her eyes.

The sky was deepening to a darker blue while splashing its sunset colours across the horizon. The sun began to say goodbye to another day while passing the full silvery moon that floated amongst early twinkling stars. I loved this time of day where day and night shared the sky for a few minutes. Fairy lights that I hadn't noticed before were quickly flickering on, shining their multitude of colours for everyone to see. Now the whole fete looked completely different and even more entertaining.

Max, Helena and I walked around playing the different games that were offered and I felt like a little girl again. Soon enough Helena waved goodbye insisting that she needed to keep her plants some company because she'd been out all day so we watched her dance between the throng of people and disappear from our sight.

"Hey Max! Where the hell you been? You've got to check this out!" a random guy I'd seen Max hanging around with before called out. Max looked down at me with a torn expression. I smiled and waved him off.

"Go, go, go I'm a big girl. There's no need to baby sit me" I shooed him with a smile.

"I'm not babysitting you Val, I want to spend more time with you" Max urged.

"I was just kidding. But you go ahead, you haven't seen anyone else all day. I was going to head back to the apartment anyway"

His lips twisted with indecision before he nodded and quickly pecked my cheek and walked over to his friend. Since our date, he hadn't tried to push me for anything more than a kiss on the cheek. I could tell he wanted more and to be more but I wasn't sure of my feelings for him. He had always been a best friend to me since day one and it seemed like he was moving too fast. Granted it'd been months since we met but I just didn't think I had those feelings.

I shook my head and felt a shiver creep up my spine. I was being far too girly for my liking. I mean, yeah I was a girl but I hated being one of those girls who constantly tried to determine all my feelings, his feelings, her feelings, everyone's feelings every damn second o f the day.

There was nothing that could give me a headache quicker!

Derrek's POV – that's right!!!

I stuffed the last bit of my burger in my mouth and chewed it lazily while scrunching the wrapper it was wrapped in into a ball. I spied a rubbish bin and threw it in an arch towards the opening and watched as it landed perfectly in the centre. Swish! I commented in my head.

I peeked around the tent I was sitting behind and saw the many different students milling around the grass. Cautiously I stood up and scanned the crowd. Thank God! Sarah had been nothing short of a love sick puppy following me around for days! Just because we were partnered up in our last Fire Skills class she somehow got into her head that we were a couple.

I thought back to the distraction contest and the things she shouted at Valerie. I shivered. Yeah Sarah had the looks and body that was hard not to stare at and not drool over but her personality killed any bit of positive thinking towards her. I mean, seriously? Screaming out that we're a couple and insinuating we were sleeping together? I wouldn't willingly touch her with a ten foot pole while wearing a quarantine suit, but I had to say that I felt a little proud.

The wind was chilly tonight and even though it didn't bother me I tugged my worn out leather jacket a little tighter. There wasn't much to do that caught my attention. If it wasn't for Val's smile and laughter I wouldn't even have played the stupid water gun game but I was able to win her something so that was a plus.

I don't know what it was about her but there was something that made me want to put my defensive walls down and let her see the me that no one ever saw. I must be crazy, or just tired. I headed back towards the campus with the image of my bed set into my mind when I saw Max bend down to kiss Val on the cheek before walking over to Chad,

I think his name was. I felt fire course through my veins at seeing Max kiss her but it wasn't my place to say anything.

Val looked after him before staring around at the people around her. Her back was facing me so I strode over to her. To my surprise she turned and bumped straight into me, her little nose poking against my chest.

"Oh, sorry Sparky" she apologised. I really shouldn't like that she's given me a nick name... but I did.

"You should watch where you're going Tadpole" I murmured. She rolled her eyes and mumbled a 'night' before walking around me towards the campus. "Hey wait..."

She stopped and raised an eyebrow as if to say 'what?' Crap, why did I say that? Tell her it's nothing, tell her to go away, I instructed myself. "Want to go on the ferris wheel? I was going to head back to my apartment but since we're both alone how about one spin on the big wheel then I'll walk you back?"

Her plump pink lips curved up into a smile and she nodded. We walked side by side towards the centre of the fete where the ferris wheel was located and I noticed her shiver slightly. Without thinking I tore off my leather jacket and slung it over her shoulders, much to her surprise.

"Thank you Sparky. Aren't you cold though?" She pulled her arms through the sleeves and I felt a like pride flare up as I gazed at the small girl in front of me wearing my jacket. She looked good in it.

I shook my head and pointed to myself. "Fire-abled remember? I don't get cold"

By the time we reached the ferris wheel the man in charge was letting people on and off the carts. We waited in line and soon enough it was our turn to get seated. I let her in first before stepping after her and the safety bar was pulled down onto our laps. Our body lurched back into the hard seat as the wheel turned slowly exchanging passengers until it slowly continued its rotation.

We were gradually reaching the top of the wheel and the stalls, games, people and fairy lights melted away below us. All that mattered was the woman next to me and the inky night sky splattered with twinkling stars and a huge silver moon that looked close enough to touch.

"So..." she whispered.

"So..." I whispered back. I don't know why we were whispering but it felt like if we spoke any louder the beauty of the night would shatter.

"Sarah huh?"

I smirked. She sneered the name as if it burnt her tongue. "Mmm" was all I answered her with.

"Interesting choice of girlfriend" I wondered if I should let her keep thinking we were dating just to see what her reaction would be but then realised it was Sarah we were talking about and I was quick to deny her suspicions.

"We're not dating. She just thinks we are for some reason"

"Oh..." I stole a glance at her and saw a ghost of a smile hanging off her lips. The ferris wheel lurched a stop making the steel bars creak and I didn't even realise we'd gone full circle and were back at the top again. The wind was colder up here and it blew lightly making Val's hair billow around her face.

I tucked her hair behind her ear and froze when she shivered. She still was yet to look at me so I couldn't tell if she shivered because of the wind or me. I didn't really care which one it was and draped my arm around her shoulders to keep the wind from her a little.

"Sparky, are all your dreams as though you're watching mine?" I didn't need to ask her what she was talking about.

"Yeah... they used to be like yours but a little different. But now it's like I just get transported into yours instead" Silence filled the air.

"I wonder why that is... do you think it means something?" she sounded a little frightened but was trying to hide it.

"I have no idea, I guess only time can tell" I told her truthfully rubbing my thumb up against her arm.

I looked down at her face and studied the angles that defined her cheekbones down to the curve of her slender neck before moving back to stare at her lips. They had felt so soft when she forcefully kissed me. I could still taste her tongue that ran over my lips.

I looked up to her eyes and saw her watching me. Her eyes were the most beautiful shade of blue that seemed so clear it felt like I was looking through a window facing the Caribbean waters. I bent my head, not taking my eyes off of hers. I wanted to taste her again.

Just as I was about to close my eyes her pupils trembled and slid into a slit. Her eyes darkened from a clear blue to a midnight murky blue and if I wasn't so close I would've sworn her eyes were black.

"Tadpole?"

She screeched loudly. It wasn't even a scream of a woman but sounded like the screech of a manic creature. Her mouth was wide open as she shrieked like a banshee and I was beginning to panic. What the hell was going on!?

"Tadpole what's wrong!" I shouted but she lounged at me, her delicate fingers thrashing around towards my throat like talons.

I grabbed at her hands pushing her back into her side of the cart using my body weight to keep her down before she pushed one of us to our death and tried holding her still. Which was almost impossible! Her strength seemed to have doubled and her face twisted and contorted with animalistic rage. All signs of Val seemed to have disappeared.

"Hey! What's going on up there!" the man controlling the ferris wheel shouted.

"Get us down now!!!" I yelled back. Luckily, the man listened when the ferris wheel began rotating again, although it was way too slow.

Val got one of her hands loose and slashed it across my throat. I felt her nails cut through my skin and I swore as I automatically held where she did damage. That was a huge mistake! She took the opportunity to kick at the safety bar across our laps and it gave way breaking apart and holding on by a screw.

Suddenly she jumped up on the seat in a crouch like a lioness and before I stop her threw her body forward and lunged at me. It was like slow motion, I tipped backwards and felt my legs leave the safety of the cart as we both fell out and towards the steel bars in the centre of the ferris wheel.

Chapter 12

Derrek's POV

Cold air rushed past my body as Val and I fell towards our most probable deaths. My hair whipped around my face and Val was still screeching and growling at me as she held onto my leather jacket. Screams and gasps of horror filled the night and every cart we fell past a blurry face or two would have no choice but to watch our descent downwards.

I twisted my neck to see the centre of the ferris wheel quickly growing closer and even though Val wasn't herself, and still trying to attack me despite our plunging into steel bars, I pulled her close to my body and braced for the impact.

My back and shoulder made contact with the ice cold, hard steel and I felt something in my shoulder snap. Instead of breaking me in half as I expected we started sliding in a spiral missing all the steel bars. The rest of my body thudded against what I thought was the steel bar and Val's head soon followed with a sickening crack. I held Val tighter to me when her body went limp and saw that we were sliding down a spiral slide made of ice. We slid onto the grass and the ice slide melted into rain before it disappeared.

"What on earth happened!?" a tall teacher, who sort of resembled a water nymph, exclaimed.

"Uh..." For some reason I didn't want to tell them what happened to Val. I wanted to ask her what the hell just happened in private. "We fell"

"You both just... fell?" she asked raising an eyebrow in disbelief. Anger heated through me, why the hell did I give a crap about what she did and didn't believe. I didn't!

"Yeah, we just fell! The safety bar was faulty. Now can someone get her off of me? I think I broke my shoulder, and she hit her head hard enough to knock her unconscious" I yelled angrily as I laid on the ground on my back with Val lying on top of me and what seemed like the entire student body crowding around me.

"Derrek! What the hell happened?!" I turned quickly at the sound of Max's voice and regretted the movement when the pain in my shoulder coursed through my body. I sucked in a breath as I concentrated on not yelling in pain. I felt hands pulling Val from me carefully and saw Coach Shulk carrying her towards the campus. I'm assuming the infirmary.

"Derrek man what happened to Val?" Max asked desperately.

"Well, nice to see you're concerned about me too" I replied sarcastically wincing in pain when he pulled me up from the ground.

"Yeah, yeah, yeah you're fine. But what happened? What happened to Val?"

"Keep your panties on, you girl. She's fine. She's just unconscious. We were on the ferris wheel and... the safety bar came off and Val panicked then voila. She nearly killed us" Once again I didn't want to tell anybody what happened and I wasn't sure if she'd even spoken to Max about her nightmares.

"Geez... Good thing Ms Flumine was there to catch you two"

"Who?"

"Ms Flumine... she's our Water Skills teacher and the one who made the slide to catch you and Val. Anyway, let's take you to the infirmary to check out your shoulder and see how Val's doing" Max said already turning to the campus.

I sighed and walked with him noticing how the atmosphere of the fete didn't seem so happy anymore.

Val's POV

My head was pounding.

I felt like a concrete truck had decided to reverse over my skull a million times. At a tortoise's pace. With an inexperienced driver. Who's drunk!

I couldn't open my eyes just yet and even the thought of trying to open them sent my head into a tail spin. I thought back to the last thing I could remember. It was night and Derrek had asked me to go on the ferris wheel. He was staring at me and I couldn't help but lose my breath a little at the intensity of his gaze. I swear he was about to kiss me, but then... that's it? All I could remember was feeling a pain more intense than anything I'd ever felt surge through every vein and nerve ending in my body, especially in my head, and then here I am.

I tried to move my hands but no such luck. They felt like lead as they hung by my side. It felt like I was in a bed though and I guess that's something I could work with.

"I know you're awake Tadpole" Derrek's deep voice stated beside my head. I jerked a little in surprise but otherwise couldn't move. "You hit your head when we fell out of the ferris wheel but the healers fixed you all up but couldn't seem to understand why you've been unconscious for the last year"

A year!?

That shocked me out of my inability to move and I wrenched my eyelids open while trying to scream 'what?!' which came out as a husky whisper. I saw Derrek in new clothes with his ever faithful leather jacket slung over the back of his chair. He smirked before laughing at me and I let him finish his rude outburst of laughter before I continued.

"I've been unconscious for A YEAR?!" Derrek shook his head and chuckle again wiping an invisible tear from the corner of his eye.

"Nah, I was just kidding. You've only been out for the night. Did you know you snore?" I stared at him. I didn't really know where to go with that.

"What happened?" I asked quietly, "You said we fell out of the ferris wheel, was that true?"

Derrek's expression became serious and he nodded looking around the empty infirmary. "Yeah, but we'll discuss it when you're out of here"

"But-"

"Later" he interrupted me.

A tall grey haired woman with thick rimmed glasses that framed her brown eyes walked through the door and smiled gently at me. "Good morning Valerie. I'm Nurse Oakley, how are you feeling?"

I shrugged, "I'm okay. I have a pounding headache though"

Nurse Oakley nodded, "Yes well that was quite a number you did to yourself. When you hit your head, you managed to split it open and had a quite a large and deep gash and you'd lost a lot of blood by the time you were brought here. Your headache should pass though"

"Oh okay. So... can I leave now?" I asked. I hated being in the infirmary. I was desperate to find out what exactly happened and it was obvious that Derrek wasn't going to talk about it until we were out of here.

"Yes, of course! Just take it easy on your head. I'd love to fully heal you sweet pea but the Abled community prefer students not to be spoilt" she winked and turned to leave me and Derrek alone.

"You heard her Tadpole, let's get out of here. I hate infirm aries..."

"Why do we ALWAYS have to go into the stinking forest Sparky?!" I groaned, as once again he led us outside and began walking into the forest.

"I don't trust empty rooms or places where people can over hear me" he answered stiffly.

"Well, I'm getting damn tired of having to come all the way out here just to have a conversation with you... I already see enough plants and trees inside my own apartment!" I complained.

He stayed silent but I saw the shake of his shoulders as he silently laughed at me. I rolled my eyes and concentrated on stepping over large roots, I didn't want to trip and face plant into the muddy ground when he already seemed to think I was a joke. We reached our emptied spot in the forest and followed him as he walked over to a tree that had fallen over since the last time I visited this place. I sat down quickly and faced him expecting him to explain what the hell is going on and what the hell happened last night!

"Well...?" I finally asked him when my patience had thinned.

"Well what?"

"Are you seriously kidding me right now? Sparky I am in no damned mood for your games!" I shouted, hearing my voice echo around me followed by the sound of fluttering wings from frightened nearby birds.

"Settle down Tadpole before you spurt into a toad..." I eyed him with a deadly expression and he rolled his eyes. "What do you remember?"

"I remember us on the ferris wheel. We were just talking and you looked at me and..." I paused. I hadn't thought over what that 'moment' was on the ferris wheel and began to wonder if I was imagining things. I wasn't sure, so I decided to skip over it, "and... that was it. I felt a splitting pain in my head and the next thing I knew I felt like I'd gone skydiving without a parachute"

"Hmm..." he voiced. He wasn't looking at me and instead seemed pretty interested in a line of ants marching over the aged tree root by his foot. "So you don't know what happened at all between those two moments?"

"I just told you. If I remembered then I would've mentioned it don't you think?"

"Well someone sure is snippy today" he said sarcastically. "Well I'll fill you in then..." He told me about what he saw happen to my eyes and how my demeanour changed. I was shocked and embarrassed when he mentioned me swiping at him and finally throwing us over the side to our most probable doom. "... then I followed Max to the infirmary. He seems like quite the lost puppy dog when he's not around you"

I ignored his jab. Max was definitely the kind of person who wore his feelings on his sleeve and made it pretty obvious to the world too. I really didn't know what to do. "So what does this all mean? I'm not some hidden transforming mutant creature who likes to come out when I least expect it"

"Are you hiding anything from me Val?" He asked suddenly. I froze at his question. For one, it seemed like lately he'd been able to tell things about me that I'd tried to keep secret and for another he used my real name. I didn't really like it.

"What do you mean?" I asked slowly, not looking at him and instead began tearing up a dead leaf into smaller pieces.

"I'm trying to help you out here, and in case you haven't noticed I'm not much a 'helper'. So have you told me everything about you that's important or relevant to your abilities and nightmares?"

He was staring straight at me, his golden eyes were piercing through mine and it was like I was standing on the edge of a cliff. It was either stand back from the ledge and tell him that he knew everything already, or jump from the cliff and tell him about my half Stinger heritage.

"How about you? You seem to know a hell of a lot about me and I don't actually know that much about you" I countered trying to steer the conversation away from me. He raised an eyebrow, obviously aware of my distraction but continued anyway.

"Okay... I'll share if you do too. What exactly do you want to know?"

Derrek's POV

I leaned backwards against the tree trunk behind me and threw my hands behind my head as I waited for her questions. I don't know why I was even doing this. I never opened up to people. Ever. But there was something about Val that made me believe that we had more in common than I'd like and I had a feeling it was something dark.

"Well...?"

"Tell me about your parents" she asked me.

I shrugged my shoulders, "Not much to tell... My dad raised me, he was Fire-abled and an ex-con" her eyes widened and I gave a dry chuckle, "Apparently my mother died giving birth to me so I never knew her"

"I'm sorry. Um... " she bit on her lower lip and I found my eyes distracted by the way her tongue licked over her bottom lip. "How did your parents... uhh..."

"How did they meet and why did my mother get with an ex-con?" I filled in for her. She nodded meekly. She wasn't the only curious one, there'd been a lot of questions as to why they fell in love with each other and I told her what I knew.

"My dad never spoke much about her, I think it hurt him too much. He met her when he was on a job. He walked in dressed up in a suit and looked nothing like the deceiving con he was and she was the teller that he held up.

"Apparently it was love at first sight and they ended up like a modern day Bonnie and Clyde until I came along. They settled somewhere isolated but when my mother went into labour I was in the wrong position and she needed surgery. Dad and mother were top priority with the police so they couldn't go to the hospital and instead went to the back alley 'surgeon' who couldn't stop her bleeding in time after cutting me out.My dad raised me ever since with a heavy heart but then died while driving drunk on my birthday, the day mother died"

"Oh my God Derrek... I'm so sorry" she whispered as a tear fell from her cheek.

I shrugged, "I didn't know her and he was an a$s. I was probably better off without them"

Val looked around the forest avoiding my eyes and took a deep breath. "I don't know how you'll react to this..."

"React to what Tadpole?" I asked curiously. She looked like a mixture of panic, fear and something else I couldn't put my finger on. Goosebumps spread across her skin and she began to tremble. I sat up from the tree trunk and looked straight into her eyes, "Tadpole, calm down. Tell me what's shaking you up so badly?"

She looked at the ground with her eyes closed breathing in deeply then slowly lifted her head and opened her beautiful eyes. Her eyes penetrated my own and then she spoke. "I'm part Stinger".

Chapter 13

Val's POV

"I'm part Stinger" I shut my eyes ready for his burst of outrage or maybe he would burn me like The Control did with my parents but I waited and waited and nothing happened. Slowly I opened my eyes and instantly caught his gaze that was set intently on me.

"So, part Stinger huh?"

Okay... I wasn't expecting that.

"Uh... yeah" I replied slowly. Why wasn't he freaking out? Why didn't he look down his nose at me in disgust and walk away? Instead of doing any of what I imagined him doing he just sat there and was apparently digesting the information I gave him with a raised eyebrow.

"Do you have the abilities of a Stinger?"

"No... I only have my water abilities, I don't have telepathy and I can't hurt anyone unless I swing a bat at their head" Derrek just nodded and looked thoughtful. His silence was really getting to me and I ended up shouting at him in frustration. "Why are you so quiet?! I'm part Stinger! You should hate me!"

"And why is that?" he asked simply. I was about to explain why when I came up short. I had no real reason. I must have been so caught up with what society thought about Stingers that I had expected Derrek to turn around and burn me alive at my confession.

"I don't know... I just thought that because The Control murdered every Stinger that every Abled hated them"

"I hate the mainstream way of thinking" Derrek explained winking at me. "I'll tell you something Tadpole. I told you that my mother died giving birth to me, and that was true, but what I didn't tell you was that she didn't exactly have an ability"

I frowned. What did he mean 'didn't exactly have an ability?'

"Care to elaborate Sparky?"

"My dad didn't like to talk about mother, when I was younger I would ask questions but would only end up getting burnt... literally. But every year on my birthday my dad would get pissed drunk. At first he'd beat me, yelling at me for killing his wife but I eventually learnt to keep away from him. Before I left him alone I'd ask him about mother and the few minutes of finding something out about her was like my birthday, Christmas, Easter and whatever other holiday put together. "

Derrek held a ghost of a smile at the thought of his deceased mom and I became choked up with emotion.

"One year, after I got my fire abilities, I asked about mother again and about her abilities. I thought she'd be Fire-abled like my dad but dad told me she was special. Mother was half Stinger and half Healer, but instead of having the abilities that came with it they cancelled each other out leaving her with no ability but extra strong telepathy"

He stopped and stared at me lifting an eyebrow as if to say 'does that answer your question?'

"So you're part Stinger then...?"

He shrugged. "I could say I was part Healer too but I know I'm not. I don't have those abilities so I'm Fire-abled" I leaned back and looked him over. He was so mysterious and now here he was telling me all about his past and his life. He'd stemmed into this cocky, confident brooding man from the abused and lonely little boy who was blamed for the death of his mother.

"So are we done sharing life stories or should we braid each other's hair too?"

And there was the mood swing.

"We're done I guess... but we don't actually know what happened to me. What if it happens again? What if I end up hurting random people?" I was starting to panic. All the calmness I felt while we were talking seemed to have slipped away and left me with nothing but fear and panic.

"I guess I'll just have to keep an eye on you then" Derrek winked at me with a cheeky grin.

I rolled my eyes and stood up dusting the dirt from my jeans, "Oh great, I feel so much safer now"

He chuckled and pushed himself from the fallen tree stretching out his arms to the sky as the kinks in his back clicked. A cool wind blew between the trees and the birds chirped from their hidden nests. I wondered why he constantly had the need to come back to the forest. It seemed that the only time we could properly talk was when we were among the trees, and I knew he said he didn't trust the rooms, but there had to be a reason? Or maybe I'm over thinking everything again...

"Lead the way Sparky" I gestured him with a wave of my arm and let him walk past. The smell of the forest filled my nose and I had to admit that it was calming. Every once in a while a glimpse of a flapping bird or the whipping tail of a scampering animal would catch my attention and I couldn't help but feel comforted by the nature that surrounded me.

"Thank God you're alright Val! Helena and I went to visit you in the infirmary a few hours ago and the nurse said you'd already left. How are you feeling?" Max asked.

"I'm fine, I had a headache when I woke up but it's gone now thank God!"

Max smiled at me as we walked through the corridors of the campus and steered me into Water Skills. He opened the door to our class and stood back letting me walk through first then followed after me. The class was already full and chatting loudly as we waited for Ms Flumine's extravagant entrance. We'd noticed over the months that the teachers each had their own exaggerated way of letting the class know they were there.

I stood beside Max and I could feel his body heat warming me as we waited in the cool room. The water in the pool rippled slightly starting like pin pricks and spreading out into rings that grew larger and larger. It began to bubble and the water began to lift into the air one drop at a time almost like the water was defying gravity.

The water droplets spun round in circles getting faster and faster until they became a blur and suddenly flew together smashing water against water. The silhouette of Ms Flumine was obvious to see but she was made purely of water, then slowly the transparent water began to change colours and the smooth liquid shifted into different textures until Ms Flumine stood before us.

"Hello class" Ms Flumine stated calmly, "As you have seen over the last few months, the human body is able to be morphed into pure water and be shifted to move with water abilities. The human body is roughly sixty percent water and therefore people with water abilities have it the easiest when it comes to changing into elemental beings. Now let's begin..."

The class was full of students with different parts of their body being turned into water then changed back to flesh. Max stood in front of me with his legs planted firmly to the ground while everything from his hips and up was pure water.

"Beat that" he stated smugly as soon as his morphed back to his muscled self.

"With pleasure" I replied with a smile. I closed my eyes and concentrated on the strands of my hair and imagined them dripping with water. I felt the coldness tickle down my scalp and drip downwards to cover my face. I let the cool sensation spread along my neck then shoulders and course out to the ends of my fingertips and stretch down to my toes.

"Whoa! Nice job Val" Max cried. I opened my eyes. My vision seemed to have a blue tinge I knew I was a complete water being. I waved my hands in front of my eyes and rubbed my hands together. It was a weird sensation to have something so tangible and smooth feel so hard at the same time I pushed my hands together and it was just the same as if my hands were made of flesh.

"Well done Valerie! Now, concentrate hard. Feel yourself mould together. You are no longer flesh, bone and muscle... you are water, and water can shift into anything" Ms Flumine's husky voice instructed me.

I did as she said and pushed my clasped hands together and smiled excitedly when my water hands meshed together into one.

"Wonderful! Wonderful job Valerie! THAT is how it's done!" The class applauded me and within a few seconds I was back to my non-water self.

"Holy crap Val you're like a freaking water ninja!" Max laughed as I grinned at him, "You're going to kick ass in Combat!"

"And so we meet again..."

Oh God... what in the hell did I do to deserve Sarah as a partner in Combat! Sarah stood across from me with her arms folded across her body. Her flaming hair was tied up in a high ponytail and she wore a white t-shirt that was cropped a little short to show a strip of her stomach and a pair of gym shorts.

"That could not have been more cliché of a thing to say unless you flipped your hair" I murmured. We'd all been paired up and I really wasn't expecting this pairing, Derrek maybe, even Colin but not Sarah.

"Whatever" she grumbled.

"Okay class! I was told you learnt about changing into elemental beings. Now I've paired you all up with a partner who's of approximately the same degree of elemental being to make it a bit more even. Wouldn't want complete elemental beings fighting against a partner who can only change their arms would we?! Let's go!"

"Hmm... maybe I'll like this pairing after all" Sarah snickered. All the students stood in two lines with each pair facing the other person and soon people were changing into their element. The majority of students were only partially morphed and so only a select few were complete elemental beings.

"Do your worst" Sarah sneered and held her hands out with her palm upwards. Fire spurted from her fingertips and began to spread across her hands burning up her arms until her whole body was made of red flames and her silhouette was blackened magma. Her hair was literally a flaming red and I inwardly chuckled at the thought. I could feel the intensity of her heat slightly burning my cheekbones, like standing too close to a camp fire.

"No need to tell me twice" I answered her. I breathed in deep closing my eyes and felt the icy cool sensation again and let it spread over me like an ice shower. I opened my eyes and everything was once again tinged blue.

I looked around and I could see Colin a few students down. He was pure rock and uselessly punching a water being and

I wondered how that fight would end. I turned my attention back to Sarah and saw she was holding a large war scythe made of solid magma with flames licking all around it. The sharp and pointed blade looking deadly even as it stood still. I focused my energy and conjured a large circular shield that connected to my left hand and a scimitar for my right.

"Please, swords are so over rated" Sarah mocked before she let out a scream and ran forward towards me spinning her scythe above her head. I stood my ground bouncing my body weight, or water weight I should say, back and forth on each foot. As she got closer she held the scythe above her head and sliced downwards to my chest.

I blocked the hit with my shield earning the sizzle from the connection and steam to rise. I kicked down at her legs and every touch and hit that connected created a cloud of steam. I swung the scimitar at her ribs and she just managed to block the majority of the hit however my scimitar was able to slice at her hand and she gasped before jumping back.

We circled each other never taking our eyes off the other and once again she pounced forward this time aiming her scythe for my legs. I jumped over as she swiped below me and jabbed the shield at her face. I could feel the solid hit of the water shield against her nose and smirked as she cried out in pain.

"You stupid Water-abled!" she screamed. Suddenly she lost all fighting etiquette and began swinging, swiping and thrusting the blade of the scythe and I hissed in pain as the blade was stabbed particularly deep into my stomach.

"I'm water honey" I mocked her, "You can't hurt me!" And with that statement I moulded my arms together joining the shield and scimitar to create a large double handed sword and lounged straight at her lungs.

Her flaming body squelched and crackled as I drove water into her fiery lungs. I pulled back and saw her collapse into a heap on the ground back in her flesh, her red hair being the only part of her close to flames. I heaved in a big breath and soon I was back to my normal self as well. Healers came scrambling forward and moved Sarah to the infirmary as they began to work on her. I was exhausted! It took a lot of strength and concentration to keep up being a water being and from all the lessons I'd learnt in Water Skills, even though it was extremely helpful, I hated having to change into a water being. It drained me too much.

I watched as Max and Derrek didn't bother with weapons and instead went for good old fashioned fist fighting. Max was a mixture of ice and solid water looking like a frosty muscled statue while Derrek was all flames and moving like a ghost.

They circled each other and every few seconds one would jump forward to land a kick or punch to the other. They became so fast they were a blur of blue and orange with only steam to accompany their fight. Their technique and power was so precise and so strong that I couldn't help but watch. I was entranced at their give and take in the fight, it almost looked choreographed!

Just as Max landed a kick across Derrek's face Coach Shulk blew the whistle and Combat ended. Students stood back from their fight and everyone was returned back to flesh. I watched silently as Max transformed back to himself quickly followed by Derrek.

"You guys were amazing!" I called out to them. Their heads swivelled to me and I waved them over to me. Coach Shulk was the last to walk out of the auditorium making Max, Derrek and I the last of the class to leave.

"I was watching you two and both your moves were so-...!" I stopped suddenly.

One moment I was overly excited about their techniques and the next I was crouched on the ground holding my hands to my head as I screamed and screamed and screamed. Pain beyond anything I'd ever felt before was crushing my skull and I couldn't help the snarl that growled out from my throat.

The last thing I heard were both Max and Derrek yelling my name.

Chapter 14

Derrek's POV

My eyes widened in shock and horror as Val collapsed to the ground and started screaming. She was clawing at her temples as though trying to rip her skin off. Could this really be happening again? Max and I were frozen where we stood but then Max shifted his weight and almost instinctively Val snapped her head up and her eyes were narrowed into slits again.

A banshee shriek erupted from her delicate throat and she bounced up into an offensive crouch. I wasn't going to be caught off guard again and I thrust my hands to my side allowing the flames that spurted within my palms to swirl and warm my skin.

"Derrek! What the hell are you doing? You're not seriously going to burn her are you?" Max shouted while glancing at me but making sure not to take his eyes off the quietly growling Val.

"Only if I need to" I answered back calmly, carefully calculating her movements.

"No! Do not hurt Val, I'm warning you Derrek"

I snorted and the fire grew a little more, "She'll be fine Max. She can be healed"

All three of us stayed still, Max and I eyeing Val as she seemed to size us up. Slowly Max brought his hands up "Val...?" Her head snapped to him and her spine arched it was almost like seeing the spirit of a tiger in her body. Max, the idiot, slowly lifted a foot and took a step towards Val and she growled.

"Max!" I hissed, "For God's sake don't move"

"No, it's just Val. Something's just wrong with her" and he took another step forward. I knew it was going to happen before it did and I ran forward to shove Max aside as Val launched herself into the air at his body and only just missing me.

"Run!" I yelled at Max and led him to the edge of the forest and desert section of the auditorium. I could hear him running after me and close on his heels was Val. We ran through the trees, bending low hanging branches backwards to fling back at the delusional girl and when I spotted a thick tree with little stubs I pushed myself faster to jump up the tree using the stubs as foot settings. Max followed after me and I was surprised when I turned to see that Val was nowhere to be seen.

"Crap! Where did she go?" I whisper yelled at Max. He twisted and turned his head looking for Val and furrowed his eyebrows when he couldn't find her either. I fell silent and listened to the forest in hopes of hearing a rustle of leaves of a snap of a branch. All of a sudden an arrow made of ice flew through the leaves and pierced my shoulder. The pain, force and surprise overwhelmed me and I fell from the tree landing hard on my back with a muted thud.

"You okay Derrek?" I heard Max's voice ask.

"I'm fine" I huffed. I focused on my anger and felt my body temperature rise wincing when the arrow melted away and the leftover water sizzled against my skin. I felt the dirt give way when Max jumped down from the tree and ran to me. He grabbed my wrist and heaved me up just as Val lithely sprang down from another tree landing on her feet as easily as a panther.

She paced back and forth keeping her animal-like eyes trained on us.

"Val... it's me Max" Max states calmly talking to her as though she was a suicide jumper. His hands were held up in front of himself and he was once again, like the idiot he was, walking towards her. "Val, you need to snap out of whatever has happened to you. You don't want to hurt us and we won't hurt you. Come back to me Val. There's no need to be scared-"

His words were cut off when Val sprang onto him. They fell with Max landing on his back and Val swung her arm backwards to swipe at his exposed throat when I ran at her and slammed against her slender body. I tackled her off of Max and lifted her over my head with one hand on the back of her neck and the other on her lower back. I threw her away from us and she landed on her ass before jumping and sliding back on her feet.

A few metres away from me in the desert scene a dirt pile shot out a burst of flames and I whipped my hand to catch it and rolled my hands together to make the flame grow bigger and bigger. All this happened in a second. I threw out my hands and the fire blew out to spiral around Val. Sweat was trickling down my temples as I concentrated on making the spiralling fire grow taller and thicker.

I saw Val's hand fly to her throat and fall to her knees.

"What are you doing to her?!" Max shouted at me.

"She won't stop attacking until something knocks her out. I'm sucking the air out from around her" I shouted back. The air around us was thick with heat and finally Val dropped to the ground motionless. I sliced my hand through the air and the fire disappeared instantly.

"Val!" Max yelled and he ran to her falling to his knees beside her. All the grass and dead leaves surrounding Val had been scorched and burnt leaving a circle of black ash. Max held his fingers to the pulse on her neck and sighed in relief, "She's still breathing"

I felt as though an invisible weight was lifted from my shoulders and I walked over to the two. Val's skin looked a bit darker and she had minor burns on her skin but nothing too bad. "Come on, let's bring her back to her apartment" I said as I bent down and slid her limp body into my arms bridal style and stood up.

"Her apartment? Derrek she needs to go to the infirmary" Max argued.

I sighed. "Max, she's barely scratched. She's just unconscious... if you're that freaking worried we'll get Kayla to heal her" He nodded and followed as I turned and walked through the auditorium doors.

Val's POV

The all too familiar pounding in my skull, as though tiny men high on too much caffeine were going psycho with axes and knives, brought me out of my sleep. What did I do last night? I tried to think back but realised that I didn't remember anything past Combat.

I slowly pried my eyelids open and silently thanked God that there was no sunlight to hurt my eyes. My skin tingled but when I looked down at my arms there was nothing there, maybe I just slept weirdly? I clicked my tongue and coughed lightly at the dryness in my mouth and throat, I felt completely dehydrated.

A light whining sound came from beside my bed and I smiled when I saw Butterscotch with her head sitting on her paws as she stared up at me. "I'm okay Butterscotch" I calmed her as I scratched her head. She yipped and wagged her tail while her little pink tongue hung out of her mouth. I was in my bedroom but still wearing my outfit from Combat and I furrowed my eyebrows when the memory of returning back here was completely absent from my mind. Eventually I noticed that I wasn't alone in the apartment, besides Butterscotch's company.

I stood up slowly noting that my legs felt like melting jello and made my way to the bedroom door and put my ear to the smooth wood. A deep voice was singing softly to the strum of an acoustic guitar and it sounded so calming and peaceful. I cracked the door open and was quite shocked to see Max on the balcony playing the guitar. He was facing the forest and singing quietly to himself and I was so intrigued and hypnotized with his deep voice that I walked out to hear him clearer without disturbing him. I tried to listen to the song and was quite surprised when I recognised it.

"We've seen our share of ups and downs, oh how quickly life can turn around in an instant, it feels so good to re-unite within yourself and within your mind, let's find peace there" Max sang the song that I was actually obsessed with when I was younger. It brought back memories of when days weren't so complicated. "When you are with me, I'm free. I'm careless, I believe. Above all the others we'll fly. This brings tears to my eyes. My sacrifice"

I felt guilty for eavesdropping on his beautiful singing so I cleared my throat and walked over to him and sat on the second sun lounger.

"That's beautiful" I complimented him. "I didn't know you could play guitar? Or even sing"

He smiled at me and continued to softly strum the strings as he spoke, "Yeah, I've been playing for years but I don't usually let people listen"

"Oh! I'm sorry-"

"No, no I didn't mean it like you were intruding. I just mean that it was something special to me and whoever I let listen to me would be special to me too" He stared into my eyes and smiled his kind smile.

I smiled back but felt that guilty little feeling nibbling in my stomach. Instead of meeting his gaze I looked back at the bedroom where I saw Butterscotch jumping up onto my bed and plopping herself on top of my pillow. Max lifted his hand and patted my knee. "It's okay Val, I know you don't feel the same way. I'm just saying you're special to me"

He continued to play the song and a few others but after a while he sighed and set the guitar aside to turn to me. "I think you owe me an explanation Val. Do you remember anything that happened in Combat earlier?"

"Combat? No... what happened?" He ran a hand through his thick blonde hair seeming to word something difficult.

"One moment you were complimenting me and Derrek then next you started screaming your head off. I didn't know what to do Val! You looked like you were being tortured by the way you were trying to claw your face off!" I frowned. This really happened? "Then all of a sudden you changed. You weren't Val anymore. You tried to..." he paused and grimaced, "You tried to kill me... and Derrek. You were pouncing on me and trying to rip my throat out. You even shot Derrek with an ice arrow!"

I gasped and held a hand to my mouth as I took in every horrifying moment that I didn't remember. Had I really done that? I felt Max's hand hold my shoulders as he turned me to face him.

"Val... tell me what's going on with you. I knew you were keeping something from me but I thought it was something like secretly dating Derrek. Not something like this!"

"Secretly dating Derrek?!" I exclaimed.

He shrugged, "You two do tend to go off into the forest a lot by yourselves"

"Max, it's nothing like that. It's just that he knows what I'm going through and we just talked a lot about it"

"About what Val?! I thought we were best friends. I thought that, as a 'best friend', you could tell me anything"

He had a point. I could tell the fact that I was telling Derrek everything and keeping my secret from Max was hurting him when he'd been kind to me since day one. "Okay... I'll tell you. Just don't freak out..."

I sighed deeply and explained all about the weird nightmares I'd been having every night, about the black outs I had and how I don't remember anything. Then finally I told him about me being half Stinger. With every explanation that I told him he seemed more shocked and then eventually looked angry.

"All this time Val. All this time you kept this from me and ran to Derrek to tell him? I don't care if you're Stinger! Being a Stinger isn't who you really are! You're kind and gentle and only use your water abilities when you need to! I wouldn't have cared! I would have listened" Max's voice was getting louder and louder and every word was filled with hurt.

His voiced dropped to a soft whisper, "We were supposed to be best friends. I knew you didn't feel the same as I did for you, but that shouldn't have stopped you from leaning on me when you needed someone"

He stood up, grabbed his guitar and mumbled a 'I need to think' before he walked to the door and left letting it softly click in place. I felt tears well up in my eyes when I realised he was right. I didn't even think of how accommodating and how understanding he was. I knew now that I thought hard about it that he would've accepted everything. Now it seemed as though I didn't trust him.

I heard the door open and close again and within seconds Helena's slim arms embraced me and I leaned in her, "I think he hates me now"

I felt her shake her head. "No, he doesn't. It was just a lot to take in Val" She pushed me a little away from her and looked at me, "Val why didn't you tell us? I would've understood. So what if you're part Stinger?"

"But... The Stinger Eradication...?"

"Val, do you remember your parents?" I shook my head, "Do you know anything about them?"

"Troy and Serena told me stories about them...?"

"And did your parents sound like good parents?"

"They were amazing parents and my dad even sacrificed himself for my mom and me" I said quietly looking down into my lap and began picking at my nails.

"And your dad was a Stinger right?" I nodded. "Then doesn't that tell you that not all Stingers are bad?"

I thought about it and realised that she was telling the truth, not just trying to make me feel better. I smiled a watery smile and hugged her. "Thanks Helena"

We moved to the sofa and just sat together in silence. Both our minds were racing with too many thoughts and I wished that I just had a switch to turn them all off. A knock on our front door interrupted our thoughts and I stood to get it.

I opened the wooden door and was surprised when Derrek stood there. "Hey Tadpole"

"Hey Sparky, what are you doing here?" I greeted him back, though my voice still sounded a little sad.

He shrugged with his hands in his pockets and leaned against the door frame, "Just thought I'd come by and see how you are. So how are you feeling? Not wanting to rip my throat out or shoot me?"

I grimaced, "Yeah, about that. I'm so sorry Sparky. I didn't mean-"

He held a hand out and was laughing, actually laughing. "Of course you didn't mean to Tadpole! I'd apologise for burning you but... I'm not really sorry, it needed to be done" he shrugged.

My eyebrows lifted. "You burnt me?"

He smirked at me and nodded. "Yep"

I rolled my eyes, no doubt he was waiting months to do that. "Come on in"

I walked away from the door and he followed after me shutting the door after him. "Hey Helena, I'm guessing you know our little friend here is half crazy"

She shot him a playful glare then giggled, "Yes, I do. But she's still the same Val"

"Course she is! She's always been half crazy, and she's half Stinger too"

I scoffed and smacked Derrek on the stomach whacking the air out of him. "So apparently I'm half crazy and half Stinger?"

He smirked and nodded. All of a sudden I got an idea, "I think I should go back home and talk this all out with Serena and Troy. They might have answers or I might find something in my parent's stuff that could answer all this craziness"

"I'll come with you, skipping university for a while sounds like a good idea to me" Derrek volunteered. "Besides, if you go crazy again I get to burn you"

"Ooh! I'll come with you too!" Helena piped in.

"I'll drag Max along. He's acting like a damned puppy that got kicked in the ass"

I frowned and felt the guilt creep back but I pushed it back. "Alright then, we'll leave first thing Saturday morning".

Chapter 15

Derrek's POV

I slammed my apartment door shut and threw the keys on the counter. Why did I just volunteer, willingly, to visit Val's god parents with her? I used to pride myself on keeping to myself and not caring about anyone but here I am hanging out with Max and his friends acting as though I belong in their little group.

I could hear Max strumming his guitar out on the balcony. Lately it'd been the same song but I didn't mind, it was one of my favourites too. I poured a glass of water and then walked outside to sit on the seat next to him. He ignored me and continued until he finished the song with a final strum of his fingers.

"So... still moping" I stated rather than asked as I drank from my glass. He threw me a pointed stare before sighing.

"Shut up Derrek. You have no idea what I'm going through. I know it's only been a few months but I really do think I love her. I thought we'd at least end up dating or something...

we're both Water-abled, and you know that people of the same ability end up together" I sighed inwardly. I wasn't the emotion sharing sentimental guy that Max was. Honestly there were lots of girls who were trying to get with him but he was hooked on Val. "Yeah, well maybe it'll happen one day" I said nonchalantly.

"She told me everything you know. She told me about what's been happening to her, her nightmares and that she's half Stinger" he turned to look at me. "She said she's told you everything" I shrugged one shoulder in agreement.

"Derrek, why didn't you tell me? Why didn't she tell me? She's the most amazing girl I've ever met and I wouldn't have cared if she was half Stinger" I shrugged again.

"It wasn't my place to tell, Max" I told him. He began plucking at the strings as he nodded. "By the way, we're going with Val and Helena to her god parent's place tomorrow. She wants to look for some answers"

This took him by surprise, his fingers stilled over the metal strings then put the guitar aside before facing me. "I'm surprised she wants me to go. I feel like the biggest jerk, I need to talk to her tomorrow" His eyes slid to mine and he frowned a little while in deep thought. "Do you like Val, Derrek?"

The question surprised me and I raised an eyebrow at him. "No. To be honest she's a pain in my ass but fun to annoy" Max nodded and yawned. He murmured a goodnight and went to bed. I looked out at the thin outline of the moon in the night sky and wondered whether the warm feelings I had around her did mean I liked her.

I shuddered and shook my head. No, it's probably just indigestion or something.

Val's POV

A wet, rough tongue licking my cheek woke me up and I groggily opened my eyes to see Butterscotch's happy face breathing onto mine. As always I was dead tired, the nightmares that plagued my sleep never ceased to scare me even though I knew everytime what would happen.

"You know, I think you're spending too much time with Helena, girl" I mumbled to Butterscotch, "You're just way too happy" Helena heard and offered me a grin but continued humming as she watered her plants. I groaned as I pushed myself off my bed and started to get ready to leave for the road trip back home. I could only hope that the trip wouldn't be a waste of time.

"Looks like it might rain" Helena noted as we piled into Max's jeep. Max had volunteered his car because it was the most spacious and even offered to drive. I could still feel that there was an awkwardness between us but I felt happiness stream through my heart at the fact that he still wanted to make me happy.

"Come on Butterscotch! In the back!" I called out and Butterscotch, who'd grown quicker than I could imagine, barked and jumped into the back of the car wagging her tail happily. "It is going to rain, I can feel the heavy moisture into clouds. If we're lucky we'll get to my place before it pours down"

"Well then let's get going!" barked Derrek. Max gunned the engine and then we were off.

We'd been driving for an hour and with every passing minute the clouds grew darker and thicker. We still had a while to drive and I was just hoping the rain would hold off. It didn't. The rain hammered down in buckets and it was almost impossible to see more than a metre in front of the car and not even the head lights could penetrate the down pour. Our chatting had stopped as soon as the rain started to let Max concentrate on driving. Lightning flashed, cracking the sky, and thunder soon followed.

"I can't see a damn thing in this rain!" Max shouted in frustration. I held two fingers up and split them apart making the pouring rain in front of the car open like a curtain clearing his vision of the road. Suddenly Max stomped on the brakes and swerved the car to a stop. All of us were launched forward only to be pulled back by the seat belts and the thud of our bodies hitting the seats were impossible to hear over the pounding rain.

"What the hell was that?!" Derrek yelled. His eyes flashed as he stared daggers at Max.

"Look!"

The road had been blocked by a huge fallen tree and there wasn't any way to pass it. "What do we do now?" Helena asked.

"Max, turn back. There's a motel off the highway back that way. We'll just have to stay overnight and hope that someone's cleared the tree by tomorrow" I instructed Max. He turned the wheel and soon we were squinting into the rain to look for the motel.

"I'm freezing!" Helena shivered as we dropped our bags into the temporary room all of us were sharing. It was a cheap motel but all we really needed was a dry place to sleep overnight. I pulled a face as we walked in further. There were two queen beds that occupied the majority of the space, a small table that held a TV, a worn arm chair and a tiny bathroom that connected on the side.

It wasn't much, even for a cheap motel, but it was something.

"I call first shower!" I yelled as I dug through my bag and dashed to the bathroom to the sound of groans of protests. The hot water pounded against my back and I felt some of the tension leave my shoulders. The run from the car to the motel was short but easily soaked through our layers of clothes. Someone hammered against the bathroom door and yelled 'Hurry up!' so I shut the taps off and wrapped myself in a thin cotton towel the motel provided.

"All yours" I muttered as I walked past a moody Derrek. After everyone had showered and all the hot water was used up we bunked down into the beds and I raised my eyebrow when I saw Derrek sitting in the worn out arm chair looking as though he was ready to sleep with Butterscotch by his feet.

"Aren't you going to sleep?" I asked him curiously cock.

"Yeah I am... but you won't catch me bunking down next to Max. He snores like an elephant with a blocked nose"

I laughed and Max just threw a pillow at Derrek's face. "Thanks man, I needed a pillow" He called out causing Max to roll his eyes. Quiet breathing began to slowly fill the room but I still couldn't sleep. I felt wound up and my mind was racing a mile a minute, I sighed and decided to take a walk. I slipped out of bed and pulled my shoes on. I stepped outside and breathed in the humid air. The rain had stopped leaving the air thick and the ground damp.

"Want some company?" I turned and saw Max closing the door behind him. I smiled at him and nodded while we began to slowly walk around the small motel. "I'm sorry about how I reacted the other night Val. I said I wouldn't have minded and you know that I'd always be there for you but I didn't do a very good job showing you did I?"

"It's not your fault Max. You were right. I really should've told you instead of keeping it between me and Derrek. You're my best friend" I told him. We found a dirty wooden bench and Max took his jacket off to lay it down for me to sit on and I smiled at his chivalrousness. We sat down and looked out towards the cloud filled sky, not a single star could be seen.

"You know I like you more than a best friend for you... but I don't want to push you. I'll be your best friend but just know that I'll always be there for you okay? I know it sounds girly for me to say so" he shrugged with a light chuckle, "but you can tell me anything. I just want you to be happy"

I felt so guilty but happy that we were making up for our argument. I leaned forward and hugged him tightly and felt his muscled arms snake around me too, I kissed him on the cheek and I felt like a weight had been taken off my shoulders.

"Come on Val, you look like crap. You need to sleep" he teased and I laughed hitting him across the head. We walked back into the room and silently crept back to our beds. I yawned loudly and soon fell asleep in no time.

I was back in the underground cave and I sighed when I knew what would happen. I stepped forward but realised the cave was different. Instead of walking into the larger cavern with several tunnels that lead out of it, I found myself standing on a cliff ledge that leaned over a huge hole that led deeper inside the cave.

Echoes bounced off the rocky surfaces making the voice seem multiplied. The voice was so jumbled together but I managed to pick up words like 'special' and 'new era'. I strained my ears to hear what the unknown voice was saying but I leaned too far and felt my body slide. My legs tipped and I was soon falling off the cliff edge into the hole of the cave.

I jumped up in shock. I knew it was a dream but that never stopped me from being scared and I felt my eyes tear up. I walked over to the bathroom and changed for the day while everyone slept and decided to grab breakfast for everyone. "Come on Butterscotch, let's go for a walk" I whispered while tapping my thigh and snapped the leash on Butterscotch's collar before quietly shutting the door to the room.

"Are we nearly there yet?!" Derrek complained. We'd been on the road for another hour and luckily the tree was moved off the road. The sun was shining brightly and only the rare white cloud was streaked across the sky.

I sighed loudly, "Another twenty minutes Derrek. Geez you whine like a baby!" I heard Helena and Max laugh loudly and we turned the music up loud and sang like idiots all the way home. We finally got home and I couldn't be happier! Derrek was so close to earning a water ball to the back of the head, he was driving me nuts! The familiar hazel coloured house came into view and I felt a little happier to be home. We grabbed our bags and walked to the house, I unlocked the wooden door and shouted as we all filed in.

"Serena! Troy! We're here!"

Serena's excited rambling met my ears and soon enough she slammed into me to squeeze me in a bear hug. She hugged everyone else, which left Helena grinning and the guys wide eyed and shocked. I guess they weren't used to such a friendly greeting. Troy finally strolled in and everyone was introduced.

"And this is Butterscotch! I found her the last time I visited home and she's just been staying with us in our apartment" Serena's lips stretched into a face splitting smile as she cooed over the golden puppy and stroked her soft fur.

"I'm glad you're here Val, but I don't understand. If there was anything that we knew we would've told you before. I'm not sure exactly what you were expecting to find out here?" Serena expressed as she continued to stroke Butterscotch's fur.

"I don't know either... maybe we can look through mom and dad's things in the attic? Maybe there's some paperwork or I don't know... something worth finding in there" I replied. I knew Troy and Serena had managed to scavenge for as much of my parent's belongings for me when I came into their care and to be honest, I hadn't wanted to look at them until now.

"I suppose. You haven't gone through them before so you could come across something interesting"

I nodded and picked up my bag. "Come on guys, I'll show you where you're sleeping" I gave them a tour of the house and dropped Helena off at my room before continuing down the hallway to the spare room.

"You guys share the spare, there's only a queen bed in there and since I know how well that went at the motel you guys can fight over who sleeps on the bed or the pull out couch" I gave them a smile and shut the door.

"So, those guys are pretty darn cute. You like any of them?" I jumped and spun around to see Serena grinning at me while she leaned against the wall.

"What are you, spying on me?" I did not want to think about her question. She shook her head and walked over to me.

"No, I just came by to see if you wanted help sorting through the attic. It's a pretty big dusty mess up there. But I am curious about who you like"

"They're my friends..." I mumbled with an unwanted blush creeping onto my cheeks.

"Mhmm, sure. Well, I'll make you guys some sandwiches for lunch and you can eat it before you head up to the attic" Serena walked off and I wondered whether she was just being her teenage-minded self or she could see some sort of bond between me and one of the guys. I shook my head and helped Serena with the sandwiches.

"Wow Val, uh... no one comes up here much do they?" Max stated. All four of us were standing at the entrance of the attic and there was a thick coat of dust that sprinkled itself over everything. Some things were covered with a moth bitten sheet that protected it from the layer of dust.

"No, I guess there were too many memories for Troy and Serena and I couldn't find it in me to look at my parents' belongings. At least not until now" I sighed. I still wasn't sure if I was ready to go through their belongings but I knew this was the perfect reason to kick me into gear.

"Well, let's get this over and done with..." Derrek sighed and he brushed past me sending tingles of heat where his arm touched mine.

I rolled up my sleeves and opened the first box I found. "It would be so much easier if we knew what to find"

We spent hours rummaging through boxes, suitcases, bags and crates. Serena even came up to help and would tell stories about the photos we found. We were chuckling at the story Serena had just recounted about her days during Combat at Abled University and we came to the conclusion that she was even worse than Helena. I chuckled as I picked up a ripped photo that had burn marks on the corners. It had that sepia look and I wondered how old it was.

"Who are these people Serena?" I asked holding the photo up for her to see.

"Hmm, these two are your parents" she explained pointing to a young couple smiling brightly at the camera, "these couples are your grandparents though I'm not sure whether they're from your mom or dad's side and this was our history teacher Mr Obsidian"

"Mr Obsidian?" Helena stalked over and peeked at the pho-to, "Val, isn't Mr Obsidian the dean at the university?" Now that I thought about it, he was. I'd only seen him a handful of times walking through the hallways but the man in the photo was definitely a more youthful and less wrinkled version of the dean.

"Yeah he is, Serena was Mr Obsidian close to mom and dad?"

She scoffed, before shaking her head in amusement. "He was quite fond of your mom. She was his favourite student, but your dad was always getting in trouble with Mr Obsidian. Let's just say that anytime they were in the same class... it would always be interesting"

"Maybe he knows something, anything about what I'm going through if he knew my parents. Plus he's a Healer so maybe his telepathy could come in handy"

We continued looking and sorting through everything and I even found an old framed photo of my parents and me as a baby. I rubbed my thumb over their smiling faces and cleared the dust that blurred the image. I couldn't help but wonder how different my life would have been if my parents were alive.

Would my personality be different? Would I see Troy and Serena from time to time or visit them rarely? Many questions ran through my mind and I had to pull the reins on them. They were questions that could never be answered because the fact was that my parents were long gone. I carefully placed the photo frame by my knee and decided that I would bring it back to the campus when we returned so I could have that little bit of a reminder of them.

It was a much shorter trip back to Abled University since the sun was shining when we left. Everyone was singing, and with a prod, or seven, Derrek even joined in. Surprisingly he had a good voice. Derrek was a little upset though that I decided to leave Butterscotch with my godparents. I just thought she'd be happier in a bigger house with a proper yard to run around in rather than my apartment considering she was alone most of the time. Serena, on the other hand, was over the moon!

"So are you going to talk with Mr Obsidian?" Helena asked when we arrived back at our apartment.

"Yes, it's the best lead we have… and it's not even a lead. But I think overall it might be helpful if he uses his telepathy on me to see what's going on"

I had decided to wait until after dinner to talk with Mr Obsidian and decided the first place to look was his office. The hallways were quiet and the clouds outside masked the bright moonlight making the grounds almost invisible except for the odd yellow lamp post. I turned down an unfamiliar corridor and was greeted with the choice of walking straight and two stairwells; one heading up and another going down.

Just as I figured I'd try walking upstairs, a flash of bright red hair caught my attention from the stairwell heading down-stairs.

"Hello again, Valerie" a sickly sweet, feminine voice greeted me.

My eyes widened when I saw Sarah's eerie smile and the last thing I saw was a fire ball rushing towards my face. The force of the throw threw me backwards and I landed on my back on the cold floor. The fire burnt the left side of my face and I screamed as I felt my skin blister and char. I felt more burning pain attacking my chest and ribs and the wind was forced out of my lungs.

My vision blurred and I was incapable of moving or doing anything to protect myself. I could feel my wrists and ankles being tied together with a thick rope that chaffed against my already burnt skin and heard Sarah's grunts of exertion as she dragged me down the stairs. My head slammed against each hard step and just before I passed out Sarah's shrill voice filtered through my ears.

"He finally found you Valerie".

Chapter 16

Derrek's POV

His evil laugh reverberated through the cave tunnels and I snapped my head in every direction it came from. This wasn't my usual dream...? Where was Val? Where was the familiar sequence of the dream?

"Well done. You did not fail me" the hiss of the mysterious man echoed through the tunnels.

"I told you I'd get her for you" a female voice replied. The voice was new in the dream and yet sounded so familiar. Their mumbled conversation bounced off the cave walls and soon it was a jumble of words, no longer making sense.

The tunnels grew to an eerie silence that was almost painful. Suddenly a shrill scream shook the walls of the cave. The scream was filled with pain, almost tortured, and I felt my curiosity almost killing me to find out. I was helpless to move, to help the screaming woman seeing as her screams echoed down every tunnel and each tunnel could probably last for miles.

"Derrek! Wake up" I snapped my eyes open feeling beads of sweat drip down my wet forehead. "Derrek, man you okay?" I could hear Max's voice and I quickly took in the familiar ceiling of my lounge room where I fell asleep on the sofa. That was by far the creepiest dream I'd had and the mysterious man wasn't even physically there.

"Yeah... yeah, I'm fine" I lied.

"You were thrashing around. You must've been having a nightmare or something"

"Or something..." I murmured while I agreed with him. I looked outside and saw it was already dark. After we got home I skipped dinner and decided on sleeping for a while but I guess I slept for a bit longer than I expected. A soft knock sounded on the door and I frowned. Max and I don't usually lock the door and the only other person who'd usually visit us was Val. Val being Val would normally walk straight in without knocking.

"Uh... who is it?" Max called out as we walked out to the lounge.

"Its- it's Helena" her soft voice filtered through the door.

"Oh, well the door's open"

Helena swiftly opened the door and was quick to close it behind her. "Is Val here?" she asked nervously.

"Val? No, I haven't seen her since we got back. You don't know where she is?"

"She went to talk to see Mr Obsidian after dinner and that was hours ago. I got a bit worried and went to his office but he said he never spoke to her. I'm getting really concerned now" She blurted out with a slight crease between her eyebrows.

"Something's wrong" I stated firmly. Thoughts of the change in my dream and the screaming woman came to mind and I hoped with everything I had that what I was thinking was wrong.

"How do you know?" Max asked worriedly.

I stared past Max and Helena at the stars that twinkled innocently in the sky between the clouds and sighed. "I just do"

Val's POV

My entire body was wracked with pain. Every single cell burned and my eyes were blurred with streaming tears. What the hell happened and where the hell was I? The last thing I remember was Sarah. A deep voice chuckled close by and I tried to see who it was through the tears. It was only then I realised my wrists were chained with shackles that kept me standing up. If I wasn't chained I'd have collapsed to the ground by now.

"Who's there?! Where am I?!" I shouted.

"I've told you for months Valerie. I told you I would find you" the unknown man hissed. I don't know what was wrong with me but I could barely see. My tears had blurred my vision and no matter how much I blinked and shook my head they didn't clear.

But then something hit me. That voice. It sounded so familiar and I gasped when I realised it was the voice of the unknown and hooded man from my nightmares.

Derrek's POV

"How exactly are you doing this?" Max asked me as we walked through the halls that Val last walked through.

"I already explained! My telepathy is twice as strong because my mother was both Stinger and Healer but had neither of the other abilities and passed that down to me" I re-explained to them, "Val is half Stinger and therefore I can sense her easier than other Abled"

I could see Max and Helena staring at me from the corner of my eye but ignored them. I could sense that something was very wrong but my telepathy wasn't as strong as I led them to believe. "Okay... Val's link ends here" I stated as we stopped between two sets of staircases in the middle of the hall.

"Link?" Max questioned, he was seemed more worried than Helena and I rolled together he was almost twitching.

"Her mind link. Her trace. I don't know what to call it but this is where I can last sense her" Geez, everything had to be so difficult with these guys.

Helena, probably sensing the tension, changed the topic "Mr Obsidian's office is up these stairs but like I said earlier I went there and he said he hadn't seen her.

"Well should we keep walking straight or try these stairs going down?" I asked.

"Where do they lead?" Max replied with a question instead of answering mine. No one answered and I guess we all had no idea. The campus was huge and there were hallways and passages that were hidden or just never used. To our surprise, footsteps sounded from the staircase that headed down and our heads turned at the noise.

"Sarah?" I said surprised to see her here.

Her eyes snapped up to mine before taking in the other two who stood slightly behind me. Her eyes were wide in shock and the slight smile that adorned her lips melted away instantaneously. She closed her emotions off and she slid a seductive smirk on. "Hello Derrek… and company" she said sweetly.

"Sarah, have you seen Valerie?" Max burst out.

She stared straight at Max with a suspicious look in her eyes but then smiled and shook her head. "No, I haven't sorry" I saw Max's shoulders slump and he stood back again. Something wasn't right, and even though I knew Sarah wasn't someone I'd like to be around, I felt as though she was hiding something and I didn't trust her one single bit. She turned to face me and trailed a finger down my arm.

"If I see her, I'll get her for you" she purred. I furrowed my eyebrows and clenched my jaws. My dream came bursting through my mind:

"Well done. You did not fail me" the hiss of the mysterious man echoed through the tunnels.

"I told you I'd get her for you"

I'd get her for you…

It couldn't possibly be that much of a coincidence, could it? My eyes followed her hand and I automatically grabbed her wrist to see rope burns spread across her normally clear palm. I growled and tightened my grasp on her making her squeak in surprise, or pain.

"Where is Val, Sarah?!" I growled and grew angrier when I could see her eyes darting down to the left and felt the pulse in her wrist racing. I already knew that she knew where Val was. "What did you do to her Sarah?" I asked menacingly.

"She already said she didn't know where she was Derrek" Helena piped in behind me.

"No, she knows. She knows exactly where Val is don't you Sarah?" I never took my eyes off of her and I could see her begin to perspire which, for a Fire-abled, was hard to do.

Suddenly as quick as lightening, Sarah yanks her wrist from my clutch and her palms are holding flames as she stands back into a defensive position. Her eyes were wild and darting everywhere for a way to escape. She knew she couldn't out-fire me. Max and Helena had seen enough and they fell back onto my flanks; Max with water rippling up to his forearms and Helena with her palms faced to the ground.

"I'm going to ask one more time... Where. Is. Val?" I said quietly. I stood tense and tall in front Sarah not even bothering to hold flames yet because I knew I could burn her to a crisp in less than a second if need be. Sarah was trembling and her flames were flickering a deep blue colour. A sure sign that the Fire-abled in question was either sad, in pain or frightened, and in this case Sarah was most definitely frightened.

"I had to! I had no choice! He made me do it!" She screamed as strings of spit flew from her usually dainty lips.

"Who made you do it? Take us to Val NOW!" I shouted at Sarah. The tortured scream that filled my nightmare had me feeling as though we could be too late to help Val in whatever mess she was in but I needed to know where she was in case there was a chance I could help her.

Tears began to stream from Sarah's eyes and evaporate as they reached her chin. Her blue flames were flickering but spreading up her arms to her shoulders and I knew what was going to happen. Just as she pulled her hands together, I swiped my arm across my body and deep red flames shot from each finger and my palm. I was too quick and too strong for her. My anger and hatred was sure proof in my red flames and my fire engulfed hers like a bush fire swallowing a single lit match.

Sarah screamed and crouched to the ground to protect herself from my angry flames and I stopped to gaze down at her. Her arms, chest and face were partially charred and she was breathing rapidly as sobs wracked her body.

"Take us to Val. Now!" I spat without any remorse whatsoever.

"Okay..." she replied dejectedly. I saw Max and Helena stand down and I appreciated them letting me handle a fellow Fire-abled.

"Max, can you cover Sarah's hands with water, just as a precaution?" I asked. He nodded and soon Sarah's hands were covered in a bubble of water, rendering her ability useless. I took hold of her elbow and let her lead us down the staircase.

The cement stairs brought us lower to an unused corridor and Max, Helena and I looked around us in confusion. This hallway seemed perfectly normal. The yellow light was dimmer down here and the hall was decorated with little statues of previous deans of the university and high members of The Control. I stared at the ground as we walked and couldn't help but notice a tinge of red that trailed along the cement hallway. Blood. That was blood that had been cleaned up that we were following and I gripped Sarah even harder, not caring if she bruised or not.

She stood in front of a statue and stopped. "Well? Unless you think Val is a made of stone and a man I doubt you've taken us to her" I growled.

"This is the very first Stinger high member the Abled ever elected" Helena noted as she read the plaque of the statue. Sarah nodded sadly and pressed one of the buttons of the stone man's coat. Heavy scraping noises sounded in front of us and the statue clicked forward leaving a thin black space between it and the brick walls.

"A secret passage?" Max asked in surprise. I narrowed my vision at Sarah and she ducked her head.

"Explain"

"This is a hidden tunnel. It was created as an escape for Stingers during The Stinger Eradication only it was never used because the Eradication happened so swiftly. There was no time to alert anyone"

"How the hell do you know this?!" I shouted at her. She just shook her head and began pushing the statue aside. We walked through and immediately I noticed the difference between the hallway and the tunnel.

The tunnel seemed as though it was carved from the stone. I seemed to head downwards and I could tell it was a tunnel that led underneath the campus. The further along we walked, the more the walls changed from stone to dirt and rocks that protruded out. Soon, we were surrounded only by dirt and rocks and flashes of my nightmares kept entering my mind.

"Where are we going?" Helena asked quietly as her head took in the narrow tunnel.

But I didn't need Sarah to answer her question... I knew exactly where we were heading.

The caves from my and Val's nightmares were finally going to become reality.

Chapter 17

Val's POV

I hung slack against the shackles with sweat dampening every inch of my skin. My clothes stuck to me from the perspiration and I was heaving in breath after breath.

"You will give in to me Valerie!" The hooded man shrieked at me. For hours he had been forcing his voice into my head and when I tried to force him out I was punished with excruciating pain, like bolts of lightning that thundered into every cell of my body and brain. He was torturing me and I didn't even know why.

I stifled a sob that escaped my grimacing mouth and screamed at him, "Why are you doing this! What do you want with me!" He stepped back and stared at me from behind his hood that shaded his eyes. I was thankful for a few seconds without pain and I gulped in fresh air to ready myself for another dose of agony. He seemed to be thinking and turned to walk around me with his decaying hands clasped behind his back.

"Fair enough Valerie. You have shown enough strength to ask questions... what would you like to know?" he hissed as he circled me like a vulture circling a carcass.

"Who are you?" I sighed. I managed to see a ghost of a smile on his rotting mouth that showed his yellowed teeth.

"Why, I'm Malum, high member Stinger and inventor" My eyes widened and a gasp escaped my mouth. Malum, the man I'd been studying in history.

"But-but you're dead! All Stingers were killed!" I retorted wincing at the soreness in my body as I my spine spasmed. He chuckled and tutted continuing his circling.

"You may be half right, Valerie. I am alive but I am nothing but a decaying corpse until I can finish what I have brought you here for" I gulped.

"Which is...?"

"To bring down the Abled" replied with a sharp hiss. If the atmosphere wasn't already dark and tense it was now. "For years The Control refused my ideas for punishment and control. For years they stood me down and turned a blind eye to what I knew was right! Now, they will see how wrong they were at their and every Abled's expense."

"What are you doing to do and why do you need me?" I whispered, my eyes bulging at everything I was hearing.

"I need you Valerie because you are special. You are a different breed of Abled and valuable to my experiment" he said matter-of-factly.

"What experiment?"

He turned to face me and slowly his rotted hands reached for his torn and matted hood. I held my breath as he grasped it and slowly pulled it back. As he pulled his hood off I took in every new bit of his face and cringed, holding back my urge to gag. He skin was as horrid as the skin surrounding his mouth. It was pale sickly off-white, which showed the tiny blue veins underneath. His nose seemed to have decayed back and looked as though it was half missing.

What shocked me were his eyes. I don't know what I was expecting, but it wasn't the black eyes with blood red irises that stared directly at me. His eyes had no white to them like that of a normal person, they were rotted black as coal. His entire face gave an image of someone caught between life and death but refused to die.

"My experiment, dear Valerie, is creating a new species of Abled. Mixing abilities and DNA to create what I call The Elementals. No more of this pathetic, weak excuse of single abilities that The Control were so ardent in keeping. You see... I've already started creating them but I need your DNA to create much, much more" Malum's eyes were crazed and his insanity was clear on his face, "Your parents defied The Control you see. As you know, the Abled couple with their own ability or with a human, this was to keep abilities strong and singular. But no more... with The Elementals I will annihilate all Abled!"

Derrek's POV

I gripped Sarah's upper arm tightly and my anger grew with every step we took. "You better not be leading us in circles Sarah"

She shook her head as she stared forward. "These tunnels are long and they're like a labyrinth under the campus" We continued and I could see Helena and Max taking in every-thing. Finally after what seemed like hours of walking we entered into a cave more constructed of stone than dirt. It seemed as though I'd flashed straight into the place of my nightmares and I breathed in deeply smelling the scent of the moist dirt and something that smelt like it was rotting.

"She's straight through there" Sarah pointed towards the entrance to another cavern, something that I already seemed to know thanks to my nightmares. She was sweating and slight trembles shook her body.

"What? You're not coming with us?" Max asked frowning as he spoke to her.

"N-no, I can't" she stuttered.

"Well too bad sunshine, you should've thought of that be-fore dragging Val down here" I snorted. I wondered what had her shaking but I didn't care, she was probably regretting bringing Val down here and getting caught by us.

I pulled Sarah to lead us through the entrance with Helena behind me and Max covering the back. Just as I thought, we entered the cavern with several tunnels that connected to it and I noticed Sarah had started whimpering and began trying to push back into me to try and keep from entering the cavern.

"Please... please let me go back" she snivelled and I raised an eyebrow at her sudden cowardice. The woman in front of me no longer had the fire inside her that matched her hair, instead she turned into a quivering, scared little girl and I sensed rather than heard that something was very wrong in this cavern.

I kept a hand on Sarah's upper arm but moved her to my side as I snapped my fingers and flames lit up the dank cave. I held the orange flames in my palm and channelled my anger through it to make it grow. The light it emitted lit the cave but left the tunnels pitch black and I sensed that we weren't alone.

"Who's there?" I shouted, hearing no answer except my voice that echoed through the tunnels.

"Derrek, I don't think there's anyone there" Helena whispered.

"No, he's right... I can feel the water in their bodies. There's more than one person hidden in the tunnels"

I didn't speak, instead concentrating all my senses on the dark tunnels waiting for some sort of movement or sound to prove Max and me right. I heard the quiet flutter of clothing to my right and snapped my head towards the closest tunnel. From the corner of my eye I noticed Max shielding Helena and turned to cover my back as he kept his gaze to the others. I was trying to listen for the movement again but Sarah's constant sniffles and whimpers were echoing off the cave walls and were too distracting to listen properly.

"Sarah, shut up!" I whisper shouted as I turned my head to face her for a second.

That second was all it took for whoever it was lurking in the shadows to attack and the next thing I knew the right side of my abdomen was burning. I cried out and instantly my hand freed Sarah who stumbled and hid behind a large rock.

"Derrek!" Helena screamed and came to my side. I held where I was attacked and quickly pulled my hand away.

"What the hell is this?!" I cried confused.

"What's wrong?" Max asked he stood over scanning the darkened cave.

"Whoever did this burnt me... but not with fire. It looks like... it looks like frost bite?" I replied confused.

"What?" Max and Helena asked at the same time.

I looked down at my burn and tried to see if I had it wrong. I know I saw blue flames hit me but the affect it had was identical to frost bite. I saw the figure move again and I pushed Helena aside just as the blue flames surged towards her. I shouted in anger as my hands all the way up to my elbows burst into angry red flames and just like a flame thrower I pushed my fire towards the strangers blue flames.

They connected in the middle and steam burst where they met. The flames lit up the cave brightly and I saw other figures hide back into their tunnels while the person throwing flames at me stepped out. I was surprised to see a tall and muscled man about our age with anger clear in his eyes. I furrowed my eyebrows and wondered why his flames were blue if he was angry.

I pushed harder and his flames died out with a sizzle then I sliced my hand across and a fire wall blocked his escape back into the tunnel.

"What are you?" I shouted holding a flaming ball in my hand. I saw his eyes darting everywhere before landing on me. He was skittish and angry and that was a dangerous combination in a situation like this. "What are you?" I repeated.

"Fire so cold it burns" his deep voice boomed and just as he finished, the tunnels seemed to come alive and figures stepped out from the dark shadows. I saw three females and another male stand in front of their tunnel and watch us intently like hawks watching their prey.

"You should not have come here. Now... you will die" the blue flame man said. I flexed the fingers of my other hand and a ball of flame ignited in that hand as well.

"I highly doubt that"

I felt Max and Helena's sides touching my own as we stood to protect each other. Max was standing tall with water bubbling up his arms with droplets hovering in front of him while Helena crouched down low with her hands to the dirt and stone.

"Kill them!" the blue flame man shouted and it was like all hell let loose!

The ground trembled as thick vines shot up through the cracks of the stone and, like giant pythons, they began snaking around the unknown people's legs trying to wrap around and capture them. Max was throwing giant balls of water that hardened to ice and I was pushing fire out like my own personal flame thrower.

But something that we didn't expect caught us off guard.

Instead of fire, water, plants or stone being aimed towards us large gusts of wind howled through the cave and tunnels while circular violet discs were thrown around and cutting through the rocks. The other unknown man suddenly disappeared and one of the females blurred and morphed into a tall black bear.

"What the hell is going on!" I cried. My mind was beyond confused and I barely had time to duck down as a flying violet disc shot over my head and sliced through the solid rock behind me.

A shrill scream reached my ears and I turned to see Sarah fall to her knees clutching at her throat. I ran and caught her and saw her eyes widen in surprise as her blood seeped through her fingers. She was choking on her blood and too quickly I saw the light in her eyes disappear as her life slipped away. Sarah's arms dropped to her side and I saw the deep gash in her throat from where one of those violet discs must have caught her.

I gently laid her down and felt my anger pulse through every vein in my body. Sarah was a liar and coward but she didn't deserve to die like that.

"Get down!" I shouted to Max and Helena and they dropped down to the ground like dead flies. I cried out as I felt every inch of my skin turn to bright red flames and I threw my hands out with my palms faced forward. Fire spurted out and stopped the strangers in their tracks as they tried to shield themselves from the heat of the flames. I looked down at Max and Helena and saw that Max had covered him in a water dome effectively shielding them from harm.

A violet disc was thrown through my fire towards me but I dodged to the side and felt my anger rise. I felt thick liquid squeezing through my fingertips and instead of flames I began to see molten lava shoot out.

"Stop!" came the cries from the strangers but I couldn't stop. More violets discs came my way and I ducked side to side like a boxer avoiding them all with ease.

"Derrek! Stop! You're evaporating all the water molecules in the air!" Max shouted. Something in me snapped back to reality and immediately my body returned to normal. I was panting and sweating and my clothes sported gaping holes throughout.

I looked over at the strangers and saw them panting for breath on the ground. They managed to shield themselves enough not to die but their skin were scorched with burns and one of the girls were throwing dirt on her head to stop the fire from burning all her hair off.

"What are you?" I shouted, eyeing each of them carefully.

"We are Elementals" the blue flame man answered.

The three of us exchanged looks of confusion and looked back, "What are Elementals?"

"We're creations..." the man spat in disgust, "mixed from the DNA of Abled and humans or animals"

"Who created you?"

"Malum. Malum is our creator" I heard Helena gasp and words of uncertainty that 'he couldn't be alive' filled the cave. I was confused and wanted more answers but only one mattered. Only one answer mattered and I needed to find out now.

"Where is our friend Val?"

"She's next..." The blue flame man answered emotionlessly and I growled in anger.

"Take us to her. Now!" I said quietly but the threat was clear in my deadly tone.

Silence filled the cave again and all of us stared the other down as we waited for a decision. He looked at the other strangers and nodded slightly. This way" he finally said. He turned and walked into a tunnel that was directly across from us and I slowly followed after him.

A feminine shout filled my ears which was soon followed by a deep yell and the next thing I felt was Max pushing me to the side as threw himself in my place. He shouted in pain and I ran to him as Helena screamed. Vines spouted from the dirt twisting and wrapping around each other to cover the tunnel behind us instantly cutting off the other strangers from us.

I looked down at Max and saw that one of the females had thrown another violet disc and it sliced through Max's chest. He was bleeding out and losing blood way too quickly.

"Max, you idiot! What did you do that for?!" I yelled at him as I tried to apply pressure to try and stop the blood, sending little bursts of flames to seal the wound. He coughed and blood splattered from his mouth.

"Don't you dare die on us!" I shouted.

"I'll...I'll try" he gasped as he tried to breathe in air.

"I doubt he would make it another half hour"

I froze.

I knew that voice. The voice was a deep hiss and plagued my nightmares for months, as well as Val's. I turned and saw the man who haunted my sleep. He'd taken off his hood and was what I imagined a rotting corpse looked like.

"Hello Derrek" he hissed, "I've been waiting for you".

Epilogue

D errek's POV

"Malum" I hissed, my voice full of venom.

His blood red and coal black eyes stared at me emotionlessly as he chuckled lightly. "You finally know who I am. It seems to be that the Elementals like to run their mouth" His eyes flickered past me to the group of Elementals and they collapsed to the ground shrieking in pain as he inflicted pain into their bodies. "Pathetic excuses of Elementals if you ask me. I gave you the easier job than the others and you still couldn't do it properly"

I glanced at Malum and did a double take, "Others?! There are more!" I cried incredulously.

"Much more Derrek. These are the rejects of the Elementals, they show too much... humanity" Malum said with a sneer in their direction.

I looked down at Max on the ground while Helena tried desperately to keep pressure on his gash. He was growing paler by the minute and his gasps were becoming more gurgled. I could feel heat travel through my body and fire was sparking at my fingertips ignited by my anger. "Where is Val, Malum?" I shouted.

"I'm right here Sparky" an emotionless feminine voice called out calmly from behind Malum. Val stepped out from behind him and she looked... empty. Her clothes were torn in different places and dried blood covered her head and exposed skin. Her face had been burnt from her left eye all the way down the side of her neck and in several other areas. She looked completely battered and dirty.

"Val are you okay!" I asked quickly, careful to keep Malum in my sight. She didn't answer me, instead it looked as though the animalistic Val was back and seething below the surface. All traces of the Val I knew, and even the emotionless Val that spoke just a second ago was gone. She was like a zombie.

"What did you do to her!" I hissed at Malum, angry red flames slowly licking from my fingertips up my fingers and meeting in my palm.

"She is my best experiment yet" Malum said. "I have brought out her Stinger powers by extracting my own essence from my mind and pushing it into her head. She is mine to control... your little Valerie is gone"

Malum had begun to pace slowly with his decayed hands clasped behind his back and I stepped in time to keep him from getting closer to Helena and Max, making sure I kept him within my line of sight and never leaving my back open for attack. "You sick bastard!" I yelled.

I'd heard enough.

My rage burst through every pore and it was though my body was no longer bones, muscle and skin but instead was made of stiff molten lava engulfed in coal red flames. "Take cover!" I screamed at Max and Helena and I saw Helena try to drag Max by the rock wall while Max used what he could to surround them in a thin layer of protective water.

I cried out my frustration and my golden eyes met Malum's red and black ones. "Now you die Malum!"

"Valerie, DESTROY HIM!" Malum shrieked while he pointed a decomposing white finger at Helena, Max and I. He spun suddenly and with a flick of his cloak he turned towards a hidden tunnel and disappeared. Val wailed and came charging at me snarling like a beast gone mad. She held her hand up in the air and an ice spear grew from her palm with the glinting point directed at my heart.

"Val no! Push him out! Push him out of your head!" I yelled, but it was no use. Val's shrieks and snarls echoed through the tunnels multiplying them over and over again as she ran towards us. "I don't want to hurt you Val but I will if I have to!"

She didn't slow down so I had no choice but to defend us. I began to shape a large curved bow out of hardened molten lava and an arrow of flames appeared on the 'string'. I pulled it back hard and released it, sending it flying at Val's shoulder. The flames slammed into her, scorching her skin and sending her back temporarily at the force. As the flamed arrow hit her it disappeared exposing the charred skin underneath.

This only fuelled Val's urge to kill.

I could hear Helena's pleas for Val to stop and Max's groan as he pushed Helena to the side to try and protect Helena. Val pulled her hand back and threw the spear with excessive force and the closer it flew towards me the head of the spear grew sharp pointed spikes. I was ready to dodge the spear but I collapsed to the ground as an unimaginable pain struck my body.

It was as though millions of hot knives were carving into every pore of my body and so much pressure was building in my head that it was close to exploding. All this happened in a second and I pried my eyes open to see the spiked spear aiming straight for my chest. I couldn't do it. I couldn't help and save Val.

I readied myself for impact. But another cry from Max broke me out of my pain induced shock. Once again, although he was sliced open and bleeding profusely he had pushed Helena aside and stood in front of me taking the hit of the ice spear. Helena screamed and dug her hands into the ground sending python thick vines shooting from the dirt to try to constrict around Val.

"Max! No!" I shouted. I ran to him and grasped the spear melting the spear easily as though it was butter on toast. All the fire of my body was gone apart from my palms. "Stay alive damnit!"

I pressed my palm to the large gaping hole below his collarbone and pressed small amounts of fire to it to try and seal the wound but it was no use. "Max why the hell would you do something stupid like that!" I shouted angrily at him.

Val's shrieks continued as she clawed at the vines tearing them apart and Helena shouted that she couldn't keep her for long. I looked back down to Max and he coughed sending blood spurting from his mouth and wounds. He gasped for breath and grabbed the front of my shirt.

"Val... Val isn't herself. She loves... you. Tell her... tell her I love her, that I'd tried do everything to make... make her happy. Even if her being happy... even if her being happy means she's happy with you" Max gasped between coughing out blood. "It's my sacrifice"

I felt tears prick at the corner of my eyes and I nodded. "You're one of the good ones Max" His face was splattered with blood and his teeth were no longer white but stained red. I felt his breathing become ragged as he struggled for another breath but within seconds his grip released my shirt and his eyes unfocused on anything in the world as Max drew his last breath.

I gently let go and stood up. No more... Max was the second person I held as they died in my arms today and it was more than I ever thought I'd have to go through. I snapped my head to Helena at her piercing scream to see Val had thrown another spiked spear at her but had struck through her thigh.

"Helena!"

"I'm okay" she gritted through clenched teeth as she sent vines to wrap themselves above the spear to slow the bleeding.

I charged towards Val conjuring up a whip of fire. I sliced it through the air and watched as it wrapped itself around Val's arms and body. I pulled it tight and the flames deepened into her skin as she flew towards me. I saw her fingers spread wide and the flames froze instantly then broke when she fisted her hand. We circled each other like lions readying for an attack. Her eyes darted all over me as she took in every move and twitch.

"Val... this is not you. This Malum's essence in your mind, push him out Val! You can do this!" I cried out as her new found Stinger powers pierced through my body and I snapped. I felt a darkness inside of me, that seemed as small as a marble, grow with each wave of pain Val sent through me. "Val stop this!" I shouted as I tried to step forward towards her with difficulty. The darkness grew and grew and soon felt tangible enough for me to take hold off.

I reached out to grab it and felt powerful. It felt like an evil strength that magnified all my powers and then some. The pain Val was pressing into me seemed to become lighter the more I concentrated on the darkness and I quickly realised what had happened. Val had awakened my dormant Stinger abilities. I stared deep into Val's eyes and saw that she was still using her ability on me yet it wasn't working as strong as before.

"Die Derrek" she hissed, yet the voice didn't belong to her. She lunged at me clasping her hand around my throat and I was shocked at her strength. She ran as she held my neck and threw me against the wall. As she choked me, ice crystals began to grow from her hand and crept to my throat and I gasped as my oesophagus began to freeze. I shut my eyes and felt the heat in me grow, melting the icicles.

I didn't know how to defeat Val without hurting her. It seemed impossible to bring her back, it was like she was lost to Malum's essence in her mind and it was slowly destroying the woman I loved. After Max's sacrifice I knew that for certain I loved Val, but there seemed no way to stop Val from causing havoc without killing her.

I cried out as Val clawed at my cheek and I used the movement to snatch her wrist and twist her so I ended up at her back. I threw my arm around her neck and held her captive and while she struggled to remove my arm I closed my eyes and gained control of that darkness inside of me and attempted to use my Stinger powers. Maybe, just maybe, I could use my telepathy to enter Val's mind and use this new Stinger ability to remove Malum's essence. It was a long shot, and I wasn't even entirely sure how to use my new Stingers abilities but it was worth a try. I had to try... or risk killing Val.

Using my telepathy I filtered through the mayhem that was crashing around in Val's mind and I was becoming more aware of just how lost Val was in her own head. I saw glimpses of the torture she endured and how hard she fought to keep Malum out of her head but then the moment when she lost the fight with him I felt the hopelessness she suffered just before her mind link disappeared and was replaced by emptiness, she became this zombie of a woman.

Then there it was.

I could sense it. I could feel Malum's essence and it was sucking the life from Val like a parasite. I waded through her mind more and I knew I was getting closer. The evil surging through Val made the hairs on my arm stand on end, like the feeling of static before being electrocuted and just as I managed to reach it I felt Val fighting me.

Not my Val, this dark Val that was poisoned by Malum's evil. Val sent bolts of pain through my mind but I kept on towards Malum's essence. It was like running through water, it was so close and yet Val was the water that kept pushing me back. I felt my frustration build and I shot it out and only realised I was shooting pain back at Val!

During her momentary weakness I thought of that torture Val went through, her hopelessness, Malum sneering as he happily tortured her, Max dying, Sarah dying... all these thoughts built up and I fired it at the piece of Malum in Val's mind and I felt the energy grow bigger and bigger. It was almost suffocating, and suddenly it exploded with such force that I felt Malum's essence blow me back like a grenade explosion.

Val's POV

My head was throbbing! It was so painful it hurt to think. I opened my heavy eyelids and saw the destruction I'd caused. Unlike the times when I blacked out, I was partially conscious of my surroundings but couldn't comprehend what was happening.

"Helena!" I cried when I spied her crying by a body with a huge ice spear sticking out of her thigh. "Are you alright?"

"I'm fine" she hissed in pain. "Are you back?"

I nodded and stuck my hand out collecting the water from the spear. "Did... did I do that?" I asked her. I was scared of what her answer would be.

"Yeah... but it wasn't the real you. It was Malum's mind making you do all that" she wiped a stray tear and glanced down to the body. I followed her gaze and I gasped holding a hand to my mouth.

"Max...?"

"He's gone" My eyes teared up and I began to cry when I saw his mutilated and blood spattered body. I was a monster! How could I have done this? I stroked his hair back from his forehead. "He told Derrek that he loved you and wanted to make you happy even if it meant that you were happy with Derrek instead of him"

I cried harder and the guilt ate at me like acid. "Where... where's Derrek?"

I looked around and spotted another body lying motionless on the ground. No... it can't be! I ran and saw it was Derrek and I kneeled by his bloodied face. He wasn't moving. He can't be dead too!

"Derrek!" I cried. I gathered his head gently and pulled it to my lap. God, I loved the man and I never got to tell him before. "Derrek! No! I can't lose you too!"